EXCELLER
SELECT

TOP PICKS

SCARS BENEATH THE SILENCE

SCARS BENEATH THE SILENCE

Real life story of a convict and his betrayal

Dr. Paromita Bhattacharya

EXCELLER BOOKS®
A GLOBAL PRESS

SCARS BENEATH THE SILENCE

Real life story of a convict and his betrayal

Cover by Tales Talks Walks

ISBN: 978-93-47397-11-0

Published in India in 2025 by Exceller Books,
An imprint of GE Group
G1, Dream Apartment, Degree College Road, Belgharia,
Kolkata, 700056, India
www.excellerbooks.com

EXCELLER BOOKS®
A GLOBAL PRESS

To my pillar of support,
my friend and comrade, my Husband.

Preface

Life has an uncanny way of weaving stories that surpass imagination. Behind every face lies an untold battle, and behind every silence, a wound too deep to heal. *Scars Beneath the Silence* is not just a story, but a journey into the fragile human heart, where at times love and deception collide in unexpected ways. This book springs from the reality that truth is often more complex than fiction. It captures the poignant tale of individuals whose lives cross in the most unusual of circumstances; where compassion is entangled with desire, and trust struggles to survive amid deception. Through the journey of a convict, a healer and the invisible threads binding them, the narrative explores how far human emotions can travel when tested by loneliness, vulnerability, and unfulfilled dreams.

At its core, *Scars Beneath the Silence* reflects the universal search for belonging. It examines how relationships, no matter how perfect they appear, can fracture under the weight of absence, neglect, or unmet needs. It is also a reminder that betrayal often begins with longing - the yearning to be seen, to be understood and to be loved.

In presenting this story, the author's intention is not merely to recount an episode of passion and pain but to invite readers into a deeper reflection on their own choices and relationships. May this journey stir your heart, challenge your thoughts, and remind you that every wound carries within it the power to heal, to transform and to rise beyond words.

Table of Contents

Chapter 1

A Stranger's Plea

1

"I don't want so much misery, it feels like my root is half dipped within the cold heart of a tombstone and I am limping my way through – half frozen, dying of pain. Every time, I trudge along the hospital floor, it feels like a warehouse of corpses with bones flying through its windows and me grappling in the pain of another wounded night... Tell me madam, what should this hapless man do to make you believe that I really need this operation, fast and quick, but I do not have the means to pay the hospital the huge sum of money it claims for the procedure! Please do not drive me away, I have none to call my 'own' in this land of yours, I am a small-time exporter of garments who landed in this alien land, your motherland. I feel like howling and crying as my life moves like a wounded wheel. Only you can set it right!"

A warm rush of blood seeped through Niyaz Ahmed's soulful eyes. Her pretty face turned crimson for a second, and even in that split second the man infront had a glimpse of her ethereal beauty. She wore a hijab, though her attire was purely official and Western. He knew his words were creating an impact on the woman sitting across the table. Niyaz had never faced such a patient before. As the head of Minaaz Banu Private Hospital, in the heart of Dhaka city, she was well-known in the medical fraternity as someone running a successful multi-speciality hospital in the memory of her grandmother who had left her loads of money and property. Though she was married to a businessman of Dhaka and into a conservative family that gave more importance to a woman as a child bearer and home-maker than a working woman, Niyaaz had her own way out, trying to balance all fronts.

Most patients who came to her hospital were well-off people and hardly anyone ever bargained for lowering the cost of treatment. If ever anyone did, the news never reached her, as it was taken care of at the front desk. This case however was different. The man in question was a foreigner, from a different country and so was sent to Niyaz. Years back, Niyaz had told her husband, Naimuddin, that she needed to do something in the memory of her grandmother, rather than just take her money for mere merriment. Naim also agreed to his wife's proposal, as with an export business he was setting up, he had no time for his family. He mostly stayed abroad on official tours, trying to expand his garment export worldwide. He knew his accomplished wife Niyaz needed some work in hand, other than sitting back home and raising children. She was educated in London and had a degree in Psychology as well as in Hospital Management. She would soon get frustrated and leave him if she was not allowed to use her degree for some good cause. Their two children were now school-bound, and the teething initial years of child care were over.

Naim had known Niyaz's family since childhood, as they were neighbours in an upmarket neighbourhood of Dhaka. Unlike many others, Niyaz was a much sought-after woman among young men, not just because of her beauty, but for her academic brilliance as well. When Naim finally married Niyaz, he was in seventh heaven, flaunting his wife before everyone, proud of his 'achievement' in usurping the princess from her throne. For Naim, she was a trophy to be won and he was happy to have Niyaz as his wife!

2

In the fall of 2004, Oluwa Femi had left the city of Lagos and landed in the capital city of Bangladesh with a wish to do some brisk business in the garment sector and keep his family income going. Before coming to Dhaka, Oluwa had been on a brief stint to India as well, an episode in his life that was somehow a well-kept secret and well forgotten.

In his youth, he had been a charming young man, a moderately popular soccer player of Nigeria. Though he never had the luck to be part of the World Cup Football team of Nigeria ever, he did get a chance to play in many national level soccer games of African nations. Unable to be the soccer hero that Nigerians usually worshipped and failing to get a chance to play in any European or South-Amercian soccer clubs, he hardly earned enough to support his family in his mid-life. He had to look out for businesses that would thrive in Africa. It was then that a friend told him about the garments business of Bangladesh and that he would get him a work visa easily to go to Dhaka and start his garment export business. By then Oluwa had crossed his mid-forties and heading to his fifties. His bones had started rattling, over usage of his leg muscles were giving way to injured ligaments. His wife Myaka was after his life, comparing his situation constantly with her friend's husband who too had been a soccer player once upon a time.

"You could not do anything Oluwa, because you were lazy. Look at Hakare and her husband, he got through in a club of Spain and works as a commentator. They earn in dollars. And look at you. Our children are now on their own, who will feed us? Even our house is on mortgage."

Oluwa knew Myaka had always been an ambitious wife. She wanted more, even if they were well off in Lagos and often travelled to the capital city of Abuja to meet his in-laws. He could provide what any middle-class man could provide, little understanding that more was needed to keep his wife happy. At 49, it was not possible for Oluwa to start his life afresh. He had to now listen to his wife, so he replied: "Yes Myaka, I have got hold of a Bangladeshi visa and will go to Dhaka to try a hand at garment export. I shall send you cheap clothes and with the help of your brother you can start a shop here in Lagos as well as at your mother's house in Abuja and I am sure we shall earn good."

But within a couple of years after landing in a monsoon-ridden country from a dry and warm African nation, Oluwa was hospital bound, for his wounded knees that often gave him terrible trouble were now in dire need of medical treatment. He tried everything, from African witch doctors who gave him concoctions of ancient herbs to cure the pain and even went to hospitals in Lagos to get modern treatment. But other than operation, no one could suggest a proper remedy. With hardly any money in hand, and with the visa ready, Oluwa plunged to travel thousands of miles and try his luck one last time even with his ill health!

3

The scent of anaesthesia and antiseptics lingered in the hospital air as Oluwa limped into the orthopaedic wing with his tall, broad frame. From there he was referred to Niyaz and doctors felt he needed an immediate operation to set his ligaments, else his limp and pain would be permanent and turn worse over months, to a point when he would not be able to walk further. He walked with the quiet pride of someone who had once run freely on a stadium turf, cheered by thousands from the stands while a soccer game was on full swing. His powerful legs had been a thing of pride for him, now betrayed by years of injury and disuse. He could hardly believe that his legs that once carried him in life would finally bow under the pressure and needed mending. Dr Riyaz said in clear words: "If you wish to walk properly and not turn a cripple get this operation done."

"But I do not have any medical insurance and not the amount of money your hospital is asking for. I cannot afford it."

"Then you can try some government hospital." The doctor was waiting for his next patient and hardly had time to listen to Oluwa's sob story. He had a knee replacement operation during the day. But Oluwa was very nagging and he kept on asking several questions to Riyaz. To get rid of this burly black man and his innumerable queries, Dr Riyaz directly sent him to Niyaz. He knew she would intelligently tackle him. After all she was also a psychologist and could see through human characters.

That's how Oluwa landed in Niyaz's chamber. In the immediate foreground he could see a bed taking up a part of the plush room, with costly paintings hung on the walls. There were also a sofa and table in the corner, probably for guests. A chart hung on a clipboard at the foot of the bed's metal frame, along with a TV set where all beds and their availabilities were blinking. High above him, an ornate, crystal chandelier on golden chains hung like a painting from a European setting. The minutely observed decor on the walls - the gilded frames of the paintings and the dark red hues of the curtains were testament to a royal taste, that of the elegant woman sitting on the other side of the desk.

Niyaz listened, torn between compassion and caution. Oluwa continued: "Maam, I have never seen such a wonderful lady my whole life, you are the epitome of grace and giving. Please be kind to a foreigner, you are the hospital owner, you can manipulate the tariff and help me get the operation done at a lower cost."

Niyaz was not someone to be influenced by sweet talk. She was used to the male gaze and appreciation from a young age. Yet Oluwa's pleading melted her heart. True he was a foreigner and they should help him, even if that meant lowering the charges. She wrote to the hospital superintendent to consider Oluwa's case and lower the cost. Oluwa's words turned sweeter, his glances longer. He told her: "You are very special. If you are ever in need of a friend, consider me. I shall always be there for you, just a phone call away, even if I return to Lagos. You deserve a good friend. I can feel it."

Niyaz smiled a bit and added: "Who said I have no friends. I have many. Anyway, best of luck for your operation."

The undeterred Oluwa said: "You might have friends, but do you have someone who will love you selflessly? You are such a lovable one My Lady, you are an angel."

Niyaz blushed and turned her face away. However, Oluwa did not miss that spectacle, even if that was for a second.

4

Within a week Oluwa was operated upon and the doctors said the procedure was a great success. With regular physiotherapy, Oluwa's limp would also vanish soon. Even in the middle of her busy schedule, Niyaz did call up his room number to enquire how Oluwa was doing and Oluwa would limp on the stick that the hospital provided him, to walk to her chamber often. He did not even knock; confidently, he would just walk in, and Niyaz somehow could never say 'no' to him. Once she had even asked others present in her chamber to leave, so that she could speak to Oluwa individually. Was it from a sense of pity towards a sick man from a different country? Niyaz hardly ever gave time even to members of her own staff other than scheduled meetings. But here was a huge burly man almost in his fifties, who was swooning over her with sweet nothings and she was loving the conversations between them. Did he successfully infringe the void within her that was building up for years in Naim's absence?

On one such day with a pounding headache, Niyaz was about to leave the hospital, when Oluwa walked in. It had been a week after his discharge and Oluwa could now walk without a stick. Like a storm, he rushed in and apologized: "Oh sorry My Lady, so you are leaving?" His call of My Lady was so Victorian in its approach and oozed so much romance in it, that Niyaz reminisced her days in England when she would go to libraries and sit with an English novel, dreaming of being the women in the stories. Hearing such words from the mouth of a complete stranger flipped a chord within.

"Oh! hi Oluwa, good to see you. How are you keeping?"

"I am fine, let's go for a cup of coffee. I will treat you."

"No Oluwa, thanks not today. I have migraine issues and have a very bad headache. Some other day. Did you come for a post op check-up?"

"No, I came just to meet you and watch you work, your lovely face, your nimble fingers that run through the paperwork on your desk, your enchanting smile when you are happy. I have come for you Niyaz. Soon I shall leave for Lagos and will miss you."

Like a shot of lightening, Niyaz stood still for a moment. Had regular visits from Oluwa turned into a habit? Else why did she feel so lonely when Oluwa spoke of returning to his country. Will she miss him too? She controlled her next step and said curtly: "Not today Oluwa. I must go home. Will talk to you some other day." Niyaz was torn between a sense of responsibility and a fierce sense of love tug that she felt towards this man.

Yet, she did not turn back. She could not recognize herself, how come a strong woman like her feel attracted towards a stranger's words? How could she be thus carried away?

The next morning when she reached her hospital chamber, she found a balm bottle quietly sitting on her table. She rang for the bearer who said: "That bottle has been sent by Mr Oluwa, he had come to pick his medical reports. He said it's a very good balm he brought from Africa, it is very effective for migraines."

Niyaz smiled a bit to herself and dismissed the man. So Oluwa followed all her details? He was so caring! Just because she spoke of her headache, here he has come with a medicine for her! Naim never even bothered about her recurring migraines, rather asked her to consult the neurologist of her hospital. She never recalled one night when Naim would massage her head and put a headache balm. She sat, opened the balm and smelt its fragrance. It smelled like wafting flowers and herbs from a land she had never been to, her heart beat to the beating of African drums as she laid back on her seat and closed her eyes for a moment.

Chapter 2

The Forbidden Yes

1

Niyaz was super busy this morning, her kids had exams and needed to leave for school an hour early. As usual Naim was in London. His garments export business was growing in leaps and bounds and that meant more work as well as more money. Niyaz's mother-in-law who stayed with her elder son in Bikrampur was subtly trying to convince Niyaz to sell off her hospital and relocate to London with Naim. They were a very conservative family and though they educated their daughters, they could not even imagine they would work outside. Many women in Naim's house still followed the purdah system and very early in marriage Niyaz realized even if she was educated abroad and wore western outfits, she would have to stick to some family norms to maintain peace in the household. Niyaz thus started wearing the hijab, read the Quran, prayed to her Allah. Naim was thus happy, peace reigned in the house specially in the first few years of marriage when domestic bliss and giving birth to their son and daughter, were supreme in the mind of the couple. They were so overwhelmed in the middle of the extended family that Niyaz forgot that she too had an independent life raised by a doctor father who was no more and who primarily raised his daughters like sons, giving them every freedom they deserved.

Her in-laws' house hence was a deterrent for Niyaz, with a very different set of rules and customs. Yet Dr Rahman had taught all his three daughters to be kind, honest, and sincere. Niyaz as a mother and wife was torn between a sense of freedom that she enjoyed in her college days abroad and the routine life of being a good mother and a caring wife. The hospital was a breather for her, where she somehow found the purpose of her life and education. She was ever thankful to her husband for supporting her and as her in-laws often mentioned 'allowing her to do a job.' Later Niyaz realized that Naim needed money she earned from the hospital as a capital for his growing garments business. Private health sector was booming in Dhaka specially as healthcare facilities were appalling in Bangladesh at the government level. Niyaz's hospital had the best of doctors, mostly educated in UK and USA and had advanced technology where different kinds of operations were done.

One day Naim told Niyaz: "Your hospital business is doing great profits. I need capital to increase my base abroad, so I am pulling out a part of the profit from last year." Niyaz kept quiet. And then replied: "I kept the profit to buy new medical equipment so that I can give better service to patients and also start the new radiology wing."

"What's the point in starting more facilities. I hope you will not stick to this hospital for long, will you?"

Niyaz could not believe her ears. "Why? What do you mean?"

"Come on, this is just a past time for you. Once the kids grow up a bit, we shall relocate to London and have a happy life there. What's left for our generation in Dhaka?"

"I do not have any such plans Naim. Do not get me wrong. But its ok, you need money for your business, I shall give you," Niyaz had said closing the book on brain therapies she was reading that night. She turned off the light on her bedside and went off to sleep. At least she feigned sleep and was actually thinking hard. What would happen if her in-laws forced her to relocate? What about the good work she was doing here? What about her father's dreams?

Dr Rahman always had a wish to start a hospital of his own, but he died quite young when Niyaz was only in school and her sisters just out of college. He did not get a chance to fulfil his dreams, a dream that his youngest daughter was giving shape to and was determined to carry forward her father's dreams. Niyaz heaved a sigh in her half-sleepy form. Within a week, with the money transferred in his bank, Naim left for London to proliferate his business.

2

A tap on the door suddenly broke Niyaz's stupor. In a second, she was back to herself and sat upright on her revolving chair. There were meetings slotted in the evening that day. She had already asked her maid and driver to pick up the children from school, as she would return late. She had to prepare a presentation to be made to the health secretary so that their hospital could get a new wing. In absence of Naim, her support system at home were her house-helps. Niyaz was expecting some hospital doctor or nurse to enter.

Instead, walked in Oluwa. Today he was dressed in a smart denim trousers and a denim shirt and looked quite energetic. The last sign of tiredness as a result of his operation had vanished and he was wearing a strong masculine fragrance that floated across the room. Niyaz got a bit conscious of his presence and gave a curt smile. A flame of embarrassment flowing through her nerves, that she herself could not recognise. These days whenever she closed her eyes, the face of Oluwa and his kind words would come floating. And here he was right infront of her eyes!

Before she could ask the reason of his presence, Oluwa suddenly strode inside the room and locked the door from inside. Within seconds he was by Niyaz's side and held her manicured softs hands in his burly ones and declared: "I am in love with you Niyaz. Do not torment me anymore. I cannot sleep at night, I keep thinking of you and only you. Your angelic face makes me mad, your doe-shaped eyes seem to look through me. I am going mad dear Niyaz, please accept my love. Let me be your dear friend and protect you."

Like a lightening striking a tall tree unannounced, Oluwa's confession of his love came as a bolt from the blue. Its burning flames almost tore Niyaz to pieces. She stood shell-shocked. Her life was already a mess from within. Though she put up a brave face, her marriage was no more a happy one. Naim was absent for weeks and months, he only called once a day and that too showed more interest in speaking to their children than to Niyaz. If ever Niyaz needed to call him, if ever she felt low, Naim usually never took her calls or even call back. Once his lady secretary even took Niyaz's call in the middle of the night and curtly said: "Sir is having a party with his friends. He has left his cell phone with me." Niyaz was never the jealous wife, yet something did not seem right at all.

Above that Naim's conservative family did not take Niyaz's working outside home well. They had lot of complaints about Niyaz, specially her mother-in-law and her sisters-in-law would call her sisters up and complain that Niyaz was not taking care of her children well. Though they did not stay with her but often dropped in at her home for a dinner or lunch and would always hold Niyaz's absence as a reason for Naim staying away from the family in London.

Her sister-in-law Ayesha even commented: "Bhabi what do you do at the hospital anyway? You are not a doctor! Why do you need to be there every day since morning? You can go shopping with me and Ammi, or even cook us lunch and invite Khala."

"Ayesha, I do not like shopping. Why don't you go and buy something for my children too. I shall transfer the money for their clothes."

"So bhabi you think just by paying the family you will get away? What about your duties as a wife?"

Niyaz would get irritated at this and at times even snapped. "Ayesha why are you so concerned about my life? Your brother is in London, how much responsibility has he taken up? From raising kids to filling in the family income, to running a business, I do everything single handed. What about you? You are a post-graduate in languages, yet you never did a job!"

"I never wanted to Niyaz. You shouldn't have also and Ammi says its high time you relocate to London with bhaijaan. Why are you staying here alone? Your parents have also died long ago!"

The mention of her parents made Niyaz sad. She missed his Abbu a lot, specially Dr Rahman had always pampered his youngest the most. He knew she was bright and intelligent. However, he passed away suddenly and that ripped the family of three daughters, forcing them to get married sooner than they had imagined. Dr Rahman was a very caring man unlike Naim and his sudden death had a deep impact on Niyaz.

3

Was Oluwa truly caring for her? "What are you saying Oluwa! I have a family, I am a mother," Niyaz protested.

"So am I Niyaz, I also have a wife back in Lagos. That does not mean I cannot fall in love. Believe me I have never seen a woman like you before and even if you turn me away, I shall always be at your service, a servant to you."

Niyaz's brain was stirring up a plethora of emotions that she had no clue how to control. Even her psychology books had probably not taught her to handle such a situation. It was so sudden, it was so unpredictable, yet somewhere within her heart she felt a soft tug, something amiss from her life, the void she had avoided so long, was that responding to this foreigner's words? She could not believe her internal turmoil raised by a stranger, as if a deep wound lay beneath for years. She had been appreciated by men of her age or within the extended family before, respected by her hospital doctors and staff, but she never was swept off her feet, no man had ever professed his undying love for her so openly. The society she stayed in was a conservative one and unlike the West, they had boundaries, specially after marriage. But here was a man who did not care about any boundary, professing a love like the ocean waves, pounding at her feet.

Every nerve of hers cried for restraint, her heart was calling for a riot of feelings, feelings that she had kept hidden for years, in the physical absence of Naimuddin, feelings that she never shared with anyone. Not even with her female friends or her sisters. She had just given herself to work and raising her children, with an occasional vacation when Naim came down to Dhaka a few times in the year. And now here was a man from another continent, someone she had never seen or spoken before, someone she had no clue about, who he was, where he came from, if at all he was the man he appeared to be! He was just overpowering her emotions, she could no longer think straight!

Oluwa realized Niyaz was feeling lost, it was so apparent in the flicker of her eyes. Without giving her another moment to think, he suddenly cupped her face in his large hands and started kissing on her forehead and then his lips rested on her eyes, soft brushing kisses like petals unfurling on a dewy dawn. Niyaz's body was melting below that burly warm hug, instead of protesting, she enjoyed the touch. For months no man had held her this way, Naim hadn't come for six long months, Niyaz never thought of indulging with any male friend.

But Oluwa's touch woke a fire in her. She had never felt such an irresistible heat before. She was somewhere losing the rhythm of her heartbeat. Then as he was about to reach her quivering lips waiting to be kissed, her urge pouting on its frame, suddenly Niyaz regained her life force. With all her might, she just pushed him away suddenly and reached the washroom attached to her room. She rushed inside and locked herself up, incessant tears streaming down her blushed cheeks. Waves of confusing thoughts swathed her partially in awe, partly in disgust for touching another man and partly as down in the bottom of her heart she was enjoying the kiss. She felt so ashamed of her thoughts. Would her Allah ever pardon her for indulging in such an association?

Niyaz took a deep breath and splashed water over her face. The tiny money plant standing on the washbasin beamed in the sunlight that was streaking through the window. This plant came as a gift from her daughter. She had given her mother a plant as she knew Niyaz was a plant lover --- a birthday gift she bought with the help of her father. Niyaz was so touched by her daughter's gesture that since then she had kept the plant close to her, in her chamber and sometimes on the washbasin to give it some sunlight. Today the plant seemed to be beaming more than usual, as if happier than usual. Niyaz wiped her tears with the hand towel, pushed her hair up and stepped out of the washroom. Oluwa was still waiting, the room was locked. Without one word, Niyaz walked swiftly to the door, unlocked it, peeped out and saw the corridor was empty. She then rang the bell on her table and called her assistant, as if she would use her like a shield against the emotions and feelings that were sending waves within her. She turned around, looked into Oluwa's eyes and said: "Oluwa, please leave. I want to be alone. I have work."

She expected Oluwa would start pleading again with her. Instead with a bowed head, the man left just with a sigh, but added before leaving: "Will meet you again My Lady, my kisses are not complete yet, your lips are as lush as the grapes of Sicily, where I worked once upon a time, your scent is divine. You are driving me away today, I can understand, but I shall never forget you Niyaz, you are my love."

Niyaz sat alone dazed till her assistant walked in and saw her lost in thoughts, a state in which she had never seen her before. As Niyaz was not talking, she thought she was wanting to know the time of her meeting. She asked: "Maam when will you join the meeting? It is scheduled post lunch." And peering deep she asked again: "Maam you look so pale. Are you unwell?"

Niyaz got up. "Let's go and grab some lunch from the canteen. Then we shall head to the meeting Mariam."

The two women stepped outside the chamber. Oluwa's strong fragrance still lingered.

Chapter 3

The Moment We Fell

1

The night was rainy, monsoon had reached the Bay of Bengal coast earlier than usual. Niyaz loved rains, she remembered her country home on such occasions, the one with lush green farms around, the house that her father had built. Now no one lived there, other than her elder sister who dopped in on weekends to look after the farmlands and the apiary they nurtured. Niyaz missed her childhood. She grew up with so much love and care around. With Naim it was all about duties and responsibilities --- they were like two poles, residing in two corners of the world, a life that had become a monotonous responsibility and not something she enjoyed.

As her children slept in a separate room, Niyaz mostly spent her nights with books or at times putting on a news channel before going to bed. Tonight, it was different. Raindrops raised a symphony of melodies in her heart. She was distracted, Oluwa's touch had somehow jeopardized her balance and the arrow of cupid bled through her heart. As she lay in bed, closing her eyes and trying to recollect the scenes ending up in the possible kiss, her mobile phone made a twittering note. A message may be. Was it from the hospital? They hardly ever disturbed her at night, other than any emergency.

Reluctantly she opened it and pop came: "I love you Niyaaz. When I was holding your hands in your chamber, I could feel the twirling of passion within me. It was all encompassing, it was so passionate, I could feel every nerve of yours twitching to be mine."

Niyaz's throat got parched. She felt a bit nervous. What was this man doing to her? How come he had such an effect on her? Should she respond? Even before she could, another message sparked: "Let me kiss your palms, let me touch your forehead and put you to sleep, if you haven't slept yet. My caress will take you to a dreamland where me and you can live."

Niyaz had no clue how to react to these passionate notes. But she was liking every moment, every text, every feeling expressed through them. She kept asking herself: 'Is it wrong in loving somebody. But what is next? What is our future ahead?'

She did not ask these aloud. Instead, she just sent a smiley. She did not wish to put him down.

But Oluwa was unputdownable. He asked like a waylaid lover: "Why are you not replying Niyaz. Can't a married man love again? I cannot control myself falling in love with you and what can I do about it? Do not torment me, I just want to be yours."

Niyaz replied: "I am a married woman, Allah will never forgive me, it is a sin to fall for you."

"Oh no, never Niyaz, God is never against love, our love is God gifted, else why did we meet? There is a divine reason for us meeting this way. I love you my dearest and I can no longer think of a life without you."

2

As days and nights passed, the number of messages increased, the number of hours spent on her cell phone staring at her screen, waiting for messages to pop up also increased. A barge of messages kept flowing from Oluwa. Mostly they had words like: "I miss you, I love you, even if you do not love me, I shall keep loving you forever."

Niyaz was very touched by these confessions of love. Even if she held herself back at times from replying as she feared that would further encourage Oluwa, but she too was feeling a strong urge to reply. No one till date had ever told her in sweet words: "Do not stop talking to me. You are a very important part of my life now." She had never felt so very belonged to another human being, despite having everyone in the family. No one ever made her feel so close.

These days she slept off with her phone by her side, Oluwa's messages sending shivers through her, that of love, that of care. She had never imagined she would start behaving like a teenager, falling in love and getting hooked to her cell phone just waiting for Oluwa's messages to blink. But the feeling kept her alive in a world of responsibilities where no warmth existed between her and her family. Everything had turned into mere duty.

Whenever her sleep broke, she would start imagining Oluwa's touch, she could not drive him away from her mind. One night, the feeling was so overpowering, the urge to meet was so deafening, that she wrote back: "Meet me for coffee at Murtaza Shopping Plaza tomorrow at 3pm."

Then she waited sometime, for a reply to come. She kept looking at her phone, yearning for something beyond just a reply. It did not arrive, Oluwa must be sleeping. Maybe he will reply in the morning. The she tried to sleep again, she was fidgeting with her mobile phone. Sleep seemed a distant dream. She was burning from a desire so deep that at a point Niyaz could not even believe her reactions. When morning came, she eagerly waited for Oluwa's message. Oluwa had told her earlier he was a fitness freak, so he got up early in the morning and every morning he would send messages to her:

"Hi Niyaz. Did you have a good sleep? How are my kids? Are they off to school? How are you, take care of your mesmerizing eyes, they need sleep and rest," --- words that would take her breath away, touch a deep chord somewhere. "How was your night?" the usual query from Oluwa. Little did Niyaz realise that's the way Africans spoke. They were open about their feelings, they never hid them. This was indeed a new experience for Niyaz. He was so caring!

Morning for Niyaz meant sending her children to school, overseeing the preparation of their tiffin, having a chat with them. But these days even the maids observed, Niyaz was absent-minded. One day she even forgot to put the tiffin boxes inside the bag and rushed her kids out as she herself was so glued to the phone that she got late. Niyaz usually drove with the kids and dropped them at their school and then headed for work.

That morning it seemed she was more lost, she was constantly checking her mobile phones. Even her daughter's words about their homework not done did not register. Then the much-awaited message came: "Eagerly waiting to meet you at 3pm at the plaza."

3

Niyaz called her maid and asked her to help the kids take a shower and get ready for school. Usually this is a work she did herself, the me-time she enjoyed with her children. Today she called Minu and said: "Minu please prepare the children for school, I have a very important meeting, I need to choose my clothes and I have no time."

Her daughter Saira kept crying, trying to draw her mother's attention. She had no intention to be bathed by Minu. Like most Class I students she was still attached to her mother, specially in absence of her father. Even her cries fell on deaf ears as Niyaz was more concentrating on choosing the best dress for herself. She always loved the colour green, being a nature lover, the colour soothed her eyes. She took out a flowing green dress and wore a matching green hijab. Then she put on an Arabian fragrance that she had kept aside only for special occasions. As she kept checking her make-up on the mirror, there were butterflies in her stomach. She even anticipated what Oluwa would say and what she will reply. She was trying to fix up her thoughts as if going on her first date ever.

As the clock struck 3 o'clock, she called her driver from her chamber, once again went to her washroom to check herself. After years, she was feeling good to be noticed, her beauty praised. It felt like she was again in her college days.

There was a lot of traffic on Dhaka roads these days, as a result Niyaz reached late. As the car entered the plaza and parked infront of the coffee shop, Niyaz saw Oluwa waiting for her in a black T shirt and tight jeans contouring up his strong legs. He had spectacles on and kept staring at the door as if waiting in baited breath for his love to arrive. Niyaz felt very happy seeing the eagerness written all over his face. That someone was waiting for her gave her a newfound hope to live and be loved. Oluwa sprang up at her sight, walked to the door, greeted her charmingly and brought her to the seat.

"How are you feeling. Hope you are not angry with me Niyaz. I will not hold back my feelings. I have fallen for you. Is loving someone a crime?"

"No, I am not angry. But Oluwa we are married, matured individuals and we have two different paths in our lives. How will they ever cross?"

"Yes, I have a wife, but I do not have a good relation with her. For years we do not have any mental and physical connect. She has a different mission in life, she is a prophetess, she goes to the church regularly, though she lived with me and we raised a family together. I respect her as my children's mother. But I have always looked out for true love that I got in you. She is my better half but I want to make you my best half."

Niyaz's face brightened up a bit. "But I have good relation with my husband. Just because you do not have a good relation with your wife, why do I have to be into a relationship with you?"

Oluwa sat a bit closer and whispered in a low tone: "Just hold my hands and look into my eyes and say you do not love me. If you say once, I shall leave right now."

Niyaz's hands were shivering. She picked up her tea cup and replied at length: "I do not know if Allah would ever forgive me. I have feeling towards you, I have no definite answer though. My husband is a good and dutiful man. I do not know why I am feeling this pull towards you."

"That feeling is called love Niyaz. Give it some time. Let us be friends. Some relations have no name. We can be more than friends."

They had tea and snacks. Niyaz could not reply. She was too overwhelmed with feelings, Oluwa's closeness, his bold, firm masculine form that oozed of care and caress. Moments made, minutes passed into hours. When the bill came, Oluwa sat still and so Niyaz paid. She thought maybe Oluwa didn't have enough money in a foreign land. She did not mind paying the bill. After all she is the one who invited Oluwa for coffee.

4

Niyaz lived in an upmarket neighbourhood of Dhaka, however Oluwa shared his residence with some more men, living like a paying guest with one room to himself. Two other men lived in the same flat, one from Indonesia and the other was from Ethiopia. They all shared the rent and hence no one had to pay a hefty sum. These days the rent in Dhaka had skyrocketed.

One day while sending love messages, Oluwa wrote: "Come over to my flat one day, let's have a chat over some juice or tea."

Niyaz was not ready to go to someone's house, but she could not call him to her house too. There were her children, maids, driver and even her in-laws would drop in and stay with her at times. Still going to a shared apartment and that too of a stranger who had turned a dear friend now, was something that Niyaz did not wish to do in the beginning. After long persuasion, finally she agreed to come over to his house. Niyaz loved the messaging, the trails of messages that she kept reading and re-reading. Unknown to her own self, she became extra possessive about Oluwa, like a demanding girlfriend. If Oluwa's morning messages did not come on time, she would call him, still lying in her bedroom: "Why didn't you send me a message today? I was waiting. Why are you late? Where did you go?"

Probably she did not even realise how Oluwa had by then become a part and parcel of her daily life. Almost after two months after their coffee date, Niyaaz finally dropped in at Oluwa's flat. He took her to his room, put the AC on and offered her a glass of juice. She sat on the bed, while he sat on the sofa. The room was quite small, and hardly had anything to look at, neither photographs or wall hangings. It typically looked like a bachelor's room. To start a conversation Niyaz said: "Oluwa, I hardly know much about you. Talk about yourself."

Oluwa looked quite excited, as if he was waiting all these days to tell her more about his own life. "I have a wife and 3 kids from this wife and one son from a previous relationship with a woman. I love my youngest daughter and miss her a lot. My wife also had a relation before our marriage and has two daughters from a previous relationship. We have raised 6 children together. My mother died young. I have a brother and sister and I take care of everyone."

Niyaz felt he must be so kind-hearted as to take in his stepchildren under his wing and provide for them. She was also a bit surprised, specially when Oluwa mentioned about children born out of a wedlock as well as those from his wife. "If you already had children and a relationship, why did you marry again?"

"Oh! The earlier woman was a witch, and my wife saved me from the evil spirits as she is a blessed person. She is a prophetess, so I married her though she is ambitious and keeps on wanting money. I married her as per African traditional marriage with bride money and all."

"If you love your wife so dearly, then why is she a prophetess."

"Well, that was her call. And now that she is a prophetess, I have asked my wife if I can have another woman in my life and she agreed. Only she said I cannot take any African woman, but a woman from another nation."

Not that Niyaz was convinced at what Oluwa was saying. Maybe their customs and way of living was so different from her own, she did not understand. She gave Oluwa the benefit of doubt. Suddenly Oluwa got up from the sofa and sat beside her on the bed and started caressing her arm. She was wearing a dress, so he easily lifted it up and started kissing her thighs. Niyaz felt so horny, she literally surrendered, her body was on heat. She had not been touched since long and never in the sensuous manner that Oluwa was touching her. Oluwa drew the curtains and then slowly he undressed her, opened her hijab too. Niyaz's long tress fell on her bare breasts. Her naked form aroused, still he was soft with her, as if she was a princess and would melt away under his power.

His slow and steady strokes aroused her even further. As their bodies intertwined, even in that AC room, she could feel the beads of sweat on her body. Oluwa was careful not to hurt her, he being a strong and burly man, took care to stroke her to a new high. Niyaz had never experienced anything like this before with Naim. He entered her finally and she reached her orgasmic climax shamelessly, her moans drowned in his kisses. The duo had not even realized when dusk gave away to an evening. He gradually lifted her and he went to the washroom first. There was a big mirror right infront of the bed. She looked into it and asked herself: Is this the man I need in my life?"

As Oluwa came out dressed in his shorts, she asked: "Will you ever leave me?"

Oluwa held her in a tight hug and said "If I leave you, why did I come to you in the first place?"

Chapter 4

The Price of Love

1

As days went by Niyaz somehow got so entangled in the 'Oluwa' charm as she always referred him as, that she started neglecting her work and even her children. For hours she would be missing from her hospital, spending time with Oluwa at his apartment, raising many eyebrows specially as she was someone who always ran around departments in the hospital and tried making everyone work to their best ability. Doctors and nurses often referred her as a workaholic. Even her personal assistant was a bit shocked and thought Maam must be giving time to her family more in absence of her husband. However, every time a problem cropped and she was called, she never replied her phone. Again, she returned to the office in a dishevelled state every afternoon from somewhere, the location unknown to anyone as these days she did not even take her car and sent it home instead. Her assistant one day asked Niyaz: "Maam are you feeling unwell? All well at home?" To which Niyaz answered in an irritated manner: "Why are you asking me such questions? Am I answerable to everyone? Just because I am missing from the hospital for a few hours, you all have a problem. Why? Are you people inefficient? Why do I always have to be sitting infront of you? Why can't you take decisions in my absence?"

No one in the hospital had ever before faced Niyaz's wrath or she did never throw any tantrums despite being the owner. She was respected by her staff as a soft-spoken wonderful boss, who always enquired about every employee and saw to it that the patients get the best care. The change in her attitude was alarmingly exposed before everyone. But Niyaz had no control on what was happening to her senses. She was so very absorbed with Oluwa, that her night and day was taken over by the knight from Africa. Niyaz was also turning possessive on him, so much so that she could not even tolerate him speaking to his wife.

"Yous said she is a prophetess and your children are all grown up. Why do you then need to talk to her?"

"Come on Niyaz, she is the mother of my children and also the garments business I run is from her brother's shop. So, I have to talk to them."

"So, you have time speaking to your wife, but no time in replying to my messages?"

"Why my love, I do reply always, don't I, My Lady?"

"No yesterday I sent you a message post-midnight and you did not reply."

"Oh! That's because I went off to sleep."

"No, you are telling a lie. You were online, I could see that from the green dot on your Facebook profile. Yet you are saying you were sleeping!"

"Then that might be because I forgot to switch off my internet. I was very tired Niyaz. We shall talk today a lot when you come, holding each other, kissing each other, promise Niyaz, I shall make up for the lost messages."

Oluwa's words would melt down Niyaz's anger to some extent, and she would again start whispering sweet nothings to him. Darkness would shroud around, the clock ticked away hours, almost landing at the entry of a new dawn, when Niyaz would drift away to sleep. But the minute she would wake up at the ring of her doorbell, with the arrival of her driver to take the children to school, she would turn to her mobile phone again. Was there any morning message from Oluwa? Oluwa often sent "Good Morning my love." On days he missed, Niyaz would turn upset and immediately call Oluwa accusing him of forgetting her. She hardly paid heed to her maid asking: "Bhabi, what tiffin to give to the children today? They are saying they will no longer eat the poori."

Nothing registered then, Niyaz would be in a different world.

2

Meanwhile Naim came to Dhaka for a week. It was one of his niece's engagements. Instead of feeling happy to meet her husband after months, Niyaz felt a bit perturbed. Her smile looked fake, s if she was trying hard to look happy and she did not even participate in any of the family gatherings before the engagement saying she had work in her hospital. Her in-laws were furious and told Naim: "See son, this is what happens when you marry a girl who is too educated. She had foreign degrees, well that was your pride. And look now, she doesn't even have the decency to be with us during celebrations."

"Come on Ammi, she must be busy turning her hospital into a multi-speciality one. After all you also know we use her hard-earned money as capital for my export business. And why I heard she has given a diamond set to Rehana for her upcoming marriage. I did not buy it. She bought it with her money. So, you know how rich she is!"

"Ahhh, that's why she is so proud and always behaves high-handed. She looks down upon us."

"Ok, ok, Ammi I shall speak to her over the weekend. Now enjoy the celebrations."

That night Naim returned a bit late with his children from Ammi's house. By the time he tucked the children to sleep, Niyaz was already in bed. Naim thought she must be tired after a hard day's work. He changed and came over to her side, touched her bare arms, and started cajoling his wife. But Niyaz did not respond. She acted being asleep, until Naim turned her face towards him and planted a kiss on her lips. Niyaz opened her eyes, something within her tensed. Why was Naim's touch feeling so alien to her? Why was she feeling tensed as her husband started opening the straps of her underwear? Why was her body not responding to his touch?

Naim was aroused by the time he took away the last shreds of her night dress. He always reached his climax fast and never bothered if his wife was also reaching her orgasm. On the contrary her newfound love Oluwa was a man of indulgence, he aroused her in slow motion and reached the shattering orgasm only after she reached her peak. Even after they had sex, he would hold her, sleep with her, speak to her in whispers and make her feel the queen of his empire, caressing her body like the feathers of an Egyptian pharaoh, tender and fragile, arousing her over and over. He would hold on to his male desire for long, fulfil all her physical need and make Niyaz feel as if she was floating in the sky. With Naim it had turned into a routine or months of abstinence as he was off to other countries and returned home only on vacations. Oluwa was like a spark, that lighted her inner flame, quietly hidden deep down.

As Niyaz stiffened at Naim's touch, her husband found it a bit weird. That night he was very tired and after the climax, he went off to the washroom and crashed in the bed. But next morning at the breakfast table, he observed his wife keenly. The children had by then left for school and Naim had told his mother that he would come over post lunch as he would visit the hospital once and speak to the board members who waited all year round to meet their co-director.

While having their breakfast, Naim saw Niyaz constantly staring at the phone. Oluwa knew her husband would be in town and was hence avoiding any contact or constant messages that they usually exchanged. Naim asked: "Something urgent at work?"

Niyaz almost jumped from her chair and said: "Oh no, nothing. Ah yes, there are some new radiology machines I am thinking of installing, so am concentrating on work."

Naim said a bit sarcastically: "And they are arriving through your mobile?" And then he broke out laughing.

Niyaz's face turned crimson with anger. But she controlled herself, deep down she was somewhere feeling guilty of cheating her husband. But did Naim also not cheat her, she was sure he had female friends in London and Hong Kong where he did business. He threw late night parties attended by his very pretty female assistant too.

She fumbled: "Well, no Naim. I am bogged down a bit with work and family, specially with you absent, so much work to do alone. Even your family doesn't help." Niyaz tried to act defensive.

"Then you better keep more helping hands. Why get so worked up."

"Hmmm, let me see what I can do," saying so Niyaz went for a bath. "I have to leave early today. See you at night, I shall pick the children from school and be at your mother's place."

As she entered the bathroom, she had forgotten to take her mobile phone. It lay on the dining table. On the screen there were 3 messages from a 'Patient O.' The name seemed so weird. Instinctively Naim tried to open the messages and read. The phone was locked with a password and he failed. But his sixth sense told him all was not ok. Something was wrong with Niyaz, though he could not understand where lay the problem. Was she angry with his family, Naim knew they were never kind to Niyaz for she was a rich, independent, educated woman and the women of his own family were mostly housewives. Hence, they had a natural disliking towards her. Or was she unhappy because of his long absence. Her eyes were always fidgeting towards the phone. The secret must have been within it. Naim told to himself: "From now on I shall come home every alternate month or take the family abroad. This cannot go on, it is not correct to leave Niyaz and the kids alone here." He thought maybe she could not cope with the loneliness. Naim felt sorry for Niyaz.

3

As soon as the engagement was over, Naim left for London. But this time he took extra effort to hold Niyaz's hands and say: "Do not worry dear, I shall come back soon. And take you all on a vacation for a month."

Niyaz was not happy at all at the proposal. She just nodded her head, half in approval. The day Naim left, Niyaz did not go to the hospital. She did not stay back home too, though her kids were at home and did not go to school that day. Instead, she called up Oluwa and fixed a meeting with him. She reached earlier than the designated time. Oluwa was still in the market. She waited at the apartment when Makanaki walked in. Makanaki was introduced to her on the first day she had been at the apartment as Oluwa's distant cousin. Seeing him, she smiled and said: "I am waiting for Oluwa."

"Oh! I see. Did not see you coming here these days. Were you out of town?"

Quite spontaneously Niyaz replied: "No my husband was here."

Makanaki looked up and said suddenly: "How much do you know Oluwa? Do you really know of his credentials and his family?"

There was a look of alarm on Niyaz's face. She replied: "Yes, why not? He told me he has a wife and many children, some from a previous relationship."

"Did he tell you that he was in India for many years."

"Well, no, but how does that matter? He has come to Bangladesh to do business."

Makanaki kept nudging her. "That's fine, but did you know what he did in India?"

Niyaz sat up. What was this man trying to tell her? Was he warning her of something? Why and what? She asked in a hesitant tone: "What did he do in India."

Makanaki somehow was not ready to tell her. Instead, he said: "Ask him, he will tell you." Saying so, he got out for some marketing. Niyaz kept sitting alone. Within minutes Oluwa barged in through the door and profusely apologized. "Oh God My Lady, you have been unnecessarily waiting for me." With one sweep, he raised her in his arms and started kissing her. He was not ready to listen to her mild protests of allowing her to be seated. He did not even pay heed to her questions: "Oluwa put me down. I need to ask you something. What did you do in India?"

Oluwa gave a deaf ear to her queries and kept twirling her in his strong arms. Today Niyaz was wearing a beautiful green satin saree with a headgear. She was looking like the

Goddess of Love and Oluwa made her feel like one too. He kissed her navel, showing through the pleats and kept twirling her, till she felt heady with a new high. They made love quite aggressively that day, as if they had missed each other so much, the urge from either side was so intense. After they made love, Oluwa kept his head on her bare body, at times twitching his tongue here and there, his sucking sounds creating a fervour within her. While professing his love he added: "I am feeling very depressed Niyaz since the last few days. Since your husband was around, I did not bother you by calling up. But my father is very unwell and is admitted in a Lagos hospital. I need to return to Lagos this Easter and talk to the doctors to find out about how he can be cancer free."

Niyaz sat up. "Oh really? That's bad news. But if you go to Nairobi, when will you return?"

"In a few weeks' time."

"So, when are you going?" Niyaz asked in a melancholic tone.

"How will I go Niyaz? I don't have money to pay for my tickets. And as you know my garments business is also not picking up. I might have to return to Nairobi for good!" He looked so sad that Niyaz held his hands tightly: "You cannot do that. You cannot leave me. Ok go to Nairobi and enjoy Easter or take care of your dad. I shall pay for your airfare. But promise you will return."

"Sure, I will Niyaz, you are my love. How can I leave you. But I shall need around a lakh to buy the ticket. Will you give me? I shall return the money to you soon. Just lend me."

"Yes, I will give you, but what about your return ticket."

"I shall manage that, don't worry, I have to return anyway. After all my lady love is here in Dhaka. I am going to Laos only for the responsibilities. You understand my dear, don't you?"

Niyaz nodded silently. Leaving Oluwa and staying alone in Dhaka would be quite difficult for her. Yet she had to let him go. Next morning in a brown packet she handed over to Oluwa the designated money. In a week, Oluwa flew back to Nairobi.

Chapter 5

Secrets across the Sea

1

Niyaz was turning restless with Oluwa away. She could hardly concentrate on any work, be it helping with her children's homework, or even her hospital meetings. She would stare at her mobile, check Oluwa's Facebook profile to see if he had uploaded any photographs with his family and wait for him to call her. Oluwa did call her at times, at odd hours, because of their time zone difference, and Niyaz would keep asking when he would return?

One day while Niyaz was trying to do some paper work in her hospital chamber, Obike, Oluwa's cousin brother who she had met in their apartment walked in after a tap on the door. Niyaz momentarily froze. Had anything happened to Oluwa? Why is Obike in her hospital? She had become quite jumpy since Oluwa left, apprehending his safety in Nigeria and if at all he will be able to return to her. But Obike smiled and sat down. With a lot of respect, he bowed his head and greeted her. "Maam I came to the hospital for some tests. So, I thought if you are around, I can meet you."

Niyaz heaved a sigh of relief! She thanked her Allah from within as she was now assured Oluwa was fine. She never these days thought of Naim's safety in London or Hong Kong. Even on the recent knife attack on the streets of London, she did not even bother to call up Niam to know if he was OK. Rather her mother-in-law called her to know about her son's safety and only then Niyaz said she would call him up and check. But when it came to Oluwa she was so over indulgent, that she always prayed for his safety. What will happen if something happens to him? She will die!

Niyaz called the hospital café and asked them to send some tea and sandwiches for Obike. After some discussions on the health tests that Obike had come for, Niyaz asked: "Obike, the other day you were asking me if I knew anything about Oluwa's stint in India? Well, he told me that he had been to India to play in one of the football clubs. But it seems there is more to the story. Can you tell me what it is?"

Obike visibly looked a bit disturbed at the sudden query. He profusely apologized and replied: "Maam it's better if you asked Oluwa yourself and hear from the horse's mouth."

Though Niyaz kept insisting, due to some strange reason Obike was not ready to divulge anything. So Niyaz changed the topic. "What about his life in Nigeria? He told me his wife is a prophetess?"

"Prophetess!" there was clear surprise on Obike's face. Rather he was quite shell-shocked. He mumbled a bit and then said: "Not that I ever heard of. He has a wonderful relation with his wife and they have three children together. And why should she be a prophetess? As a family man they raise the kids together, even the ones from their earlier marriages and they have a good sexual relationship also. You know how sexy Nigerian men are!" saying so Obike winked and gave a mischievous smile. For Niyaz these new revelations sucked all the remaining happiness and threw her into a vortex of probable lies and deception. She grew even more inquisitive and started asking more questions.

2

"What about his football clubs? He was a big player in Nigeria?"

Obike shook his head and said: "Come on, madam, in Nigeria every second male is a footballer. But there are very few who make it to the national league. Only they become players. Rest turn into managers, managing smaller soccer clubs. And people like Oluwa throw around their weight as soccer players to those like you who have no clue about the game."

Niyaz shifted in her chair. "What do you mean?" She was visibly feeling shaken. She did not know how to react.

"Why? Didn't Oluwa tell you where he played?"

"Yes, he said he played in some club in Goa."

"Huh! Goa! Well, that was the place where he met Alvita."

Niyaz's curiosity now shot through the roof. Who was this woman. That's not the name of his wife. "Who is Alvita?" she enquired.

"Alvita is a Goanese Christian woman. While in Goa, though Oluwa was married and his wife having their second child, Oluwa got into a deep affair with this girl and even promised her that he would marry her. But her father was against the daughter marrying a Nigerian and stopped Alvita at the right time. Else Oluwa would have had two wives at a time, one at home and one in India."

Niyaz could not believe her ears. Spontaneously words came out through her mouth: "So he was two timing?"

Obike looked up. "Well, you probably have no idea about our customs. We can have lovers and wives and our women do not worry much about that. And Oluwa had another woman also named Kibe. He was flirting with her too, though Kibe was African and did not mind an affair with a married man. Are you surprised maam?"

Obike could clearly see how very shaken Niyaz looked. Her fair face turned pale and she had a distant look in her eyes.

"Obike tell me more, will you?"

"I must get up maam, I shall get late for my meeting. Thanks for the tea and sandwiches. But next time you meet Oluwa do ask about India," saying so Obike did not wait for Niyaz to reply. He rushed out of the office leaving behind a visibly dazed Niyaz at the table.

Her daze broke as he mobile started ringing incessantly. She looked at it hurriedly, imagining Oluwa was calling. After all the time had come for him to return. Two weeks already gone. Instead, she found Naim calling. She took the call and could hear an apprehensive voice: "All ok Niyaz? Why did you take such a long time to take my call? Where have you been?"

"I was working Naim. Am at the hospital, don't you know I remain very busy here? How can you expect I shall pick up as soon as you dial?"

She sounded irritated. Naim mellowed a bit: "Niyaz I am not expecting that, but there was a time when you called me every day. These days you don't even call. I am not complaining, but still are you so busy that you cannot call me or take my calls? Is something wrong?"

"What should be wrong?" there was a challenging tone in Niyaz's voice.

"How will I know? But if you are feeling overwhelmed, come over to London with the kids and spend some time here. You will feel good."

"What made you think I am overwhelmed or something is bothering me?" Again, there was a hint of irritation. Naim thought best not to bother her in the middle of her work. Something was odd somewhere. Naim could feel it, but did not understand what it was! Rather he felt guilty that he left his wife and children in Dhaka to pursue his business interest in other countries and could not give much time to anyone, even his Ammi was complaining the other day.

3

That night after dinner, her children wanted Niyaz to read out stories to them. But she had no time even for them, she did not feel like, and asked her maid to put the children to sleep much to their protests. She paid no heed. Like a woman in trance, she crashed on her bed and started checking Oluwa's Instagram account for photographs of Nigeria. Oluwa had told her they lived in a big city and they had a house, and belonged to a big local tribe. She was curious to know more. And just then popped a smiling Oluwa with his wife on his lap, cuddling sensuously with their friends around holding glasses of alcohol. Niyaz checked the posting date and found it was just the day before. She turned angry and immediately called Oluwa on a Whatsup call. The phone kept ringing. She almost banged the phone down and tears rolled down. Why was she crying? Wasn't she acting like a teenager? But why did Oluwa say he had no relation with his wife? Here he was very much enjoying with his wife, kissing, hugging and with all sorts of explicit loving images.

She dozed off when suddenly Oluwa's call came in and like a shaken leaf, with a jolt she sat up and took the call. Oluwa drooled on the other side: "Hellooooooo, sweetheart, how are you?"

"So, you are enjoying with your wife and posting lovey-dovey photos!"

A bit of silence at the other end prompted her to shout more and say: "You said your wife is a prophetess and here I find you with her sitting on your lap."

Oluwa said in a calm voice: "Oh dearest, you are my love, she is my responsibility. Do you not have ex with your husband when he is in Dhaka? We have to keep up this face, isn't it?"

Niyaz calmed down a bit and she shot the next query: "When are you returning."

"Next week for sure."

"No give me the date."

"I do not have my tickets done, I spent so much buying things for the house and the children that I have no money left."

"What!" Niyaz shouted again. "So, you have no plans to come down."

"I have no money left Niyaz."

Without thinking twice, Niyaz said: "Then I am sending you tickets, or the money through international wire. You have to come."

"Ok My Lady, if you say so. Yes, I too wish to come, haven't seen you for so long. I miss you dear."

Niyaz's heart melted a bit. "Oluwa let's go on a trip together. I have to go to Chittagong by the end of this month. Why don't you accompany me? By then you will be landing in Dhaka."

"Oh, sure sure, why not. After work we shall make love and I shall feed you lovely Nigerian dishes. I have also bought some tribal ornaments for you from Lusaka. I am dying to meet you dear. Send me the tickets and kissing you good night. Have a great sleep. How are my children?"

After another few minutes of conversation, finally Niyaz left. Next day she would send him the money for the tickets and also book the Chittagong hotel. She had to do it herself as her secretary shouldn't know that she was booking for double occupancy. That night Niyaz dreamt of Oluwa landing at the airport and she rushing into his welcoming arms. Niyaz smiled in her dreams --- an indulgent lovely smile.

Chapter 6

Fractured Trust

1

It had been almost a week that Oluwa landed in Dhaka, keeping his words to return soon. Niyaz felt happy again, despite all the suspicions planted deep in her mind after her conversation with Obike. Several unanswered queries kept hovering, she surely needed answers to all of them. Keeping those queries aside, Niyaz had been to the airport to pick up Oluwa. She did not take her own car, fearing that might make people suspicious and took an Uber. Oluwa hugged her warmly after leaving the airport gates and held her like a long-lost friend, as if meeting after decades. All of Niyaz's ire, anger, suspicions seemed to melt away in that moment of togetherness. Oluwa had a sort of tender touch that made Niyaz hard to believe that this man could ever do anything wrong.

Once they left the airport gates and entered the waiting Uber booked by Niyaz, she said: "I am going to Chittagong on work next week. Will you join me?"

Within a second Oluwa ecstatically replied: "Surely my love, anything for you."

"I think some time together, will help sort out things."

"What things Niyaz?" Oluwa's voice was a bit guarded.

In a matter-of-fact manner Niyaz replied: "Nothing much, but I need you to be with me, to discuss, to talk, to vent out."

Oluwa added: "And also to make love. I shall make some great Nigerian dishes for you that I learnt this time."

Niyaz turned to him suddenly with an alarming query in her eyes: "Oluwa tell me something, how many women do you have or had in your life?"

"Ahh, my lady, I had some, you know, but if you ask me, you are the only one, I ever loved."

"I think you are avoiding my question Oluwa. You must have had intimate relationship with many women like me."

"Never never, My Lady. Believe me. Yes, I did have some flings once or twice, one-night stands, sleeping with a couple of prostitutes, but nothing serious. In our country society is not like yours, we are very liberal, our women also do not mind physical intimacy without any commitment."

"Then how come you married? Didn't your wife mind you having relations with others?"

"Oh, we had to marry as our families wanted us to. My wife got pregnant before marriage and we were pressurized into having a formal traditional marriage. But believe me Niyaz I never could love her, I had to put up the show, after all we have kids together. And in Nigeria we believe those belonging to the same tribe has a sort of responsibility towards others. We never abandon people. You are special to me dear."

"So, who am I in your life Oluwa in the middle of these multiple women?" Niyaz's voice sounded quite sentimental.

"Oh, you are my queen. You are the only one I adore," saying so Oluwa held her hands tight. Niyaz felt like taking them away in one shove, something within was seething in subdued anger. But she let Oluwa fondle with her soft fingers.

"Why were you in India?"

For a split second, the direct query came as a shot to Oluwa but he gathered himself and drooled and said: "I told you I used to play in the Indian clubs. First in Goa and then later in Kolkata."

"You never said you were in Kolkata."

"Oh! that was a brief stint. I will tell you someday."

"Why not now?"

"Come on Niyaz, let's prepare for our vacation to Chittagong. We shall have enough time later to talk. I am not going anywhere, I shall always be with you."

2

Chittagong came as a bliss, not just the distant blue hills that reminded Niyaz of the first trip she made with Naim outside Bangladesh to the hill stations of North Bengal in India, but the sea at Cox Bazar, was a refreshing break. She had told her family and Naim that she was going on work, to find out if they can start a branch of their hospital in Chittagong. There were indeed some investors who had shown interest in starting a chain of medical centres with her help. Naim was not too keen with the proposal as that meant Niyaz would get more hooked to Bangladesh and refuse to leave. But he was worried a bit, Niyaz's attitude seemed so defiant and distant these days, that negating her thoughts might create a further rift. Naim being an intelligent man instead of trying to put a stop to her hospital expansion plans, only gave some practical inputs when Niyaz called him one day to inform she was going to Chittagong on work for a week.

"Niyaz, can you handle so much at a time? I am not there to help you."

"Yes, I can, let me speak to the investors and speaking to them doesn't mean I am starting the centre there. No harm in having a preliminary talk."

"Well, that you can do on zoom."

"Yes, I can, but I want to go to Chittagong, I like the hills and the sea. I need rest away from family too."

"Then why not take your secretary along, she can help with the work too and look after you."

Niyaz stiffened a bit. Was Naim suspicious of her going alone? "No Naim, she has lots of work here in my absence."

"What about the kids? Who are they staying with? Ammi is out of town too, gone to the village."

"I know, I have made arrangements. My mother and sister will stay with them. You don't worry. They will be taken care of." Niyaz's tone was so professional! Naim could not believe his ears. Still, he did not bother her further, though he had a wish to ask which hotel she was putting up in! He would ask her secretary instead.

Niyaz always covered her tracks well. She did not book any hotel, instead she booked an apartment through an online portal, so that her secretary was no way involved and none would know she had a companion with her.

The trip was indeed fun and Oluwa made wonderful dishes for dinner and waited up for her when she returned from meetings. One day, Oluwa made the Nigerian traditional dish of 'Pate.' He knew Niyaz loved her rice a lot and this dish combined rice with ground dry corn, spinach, tomatoes, onion, peppers, garden eggs, locust beans, groundnuts, biscuit bones, and minced meat. He had been to the supermarket with the money that Niyaz left in the drawer and bought whatever was needed. He was undoubtedly out to impress Niyaz with his culinary skills.

When Niyaz returned, he presented the meal to her: "This is one of the most iconic foods in Nigeria and is eaten in every part of our country."

Niyaz was tired, but this was the first time a man was preparing food for her. She was very impressed. She could never imagine herself returning home from work and Naim making a dish for her. Infact, in Bangladesh men hardly knew how to cook as the kitchen was considered to be a place where women belonged. But when she was studying abroad, Niyaz had seen many of her male classmates, whipping up dishes when they were on a sleep over or even in someone's house. After years, here was a man kindly preparing a meal, and that too a sumptuous looking dish for her. Niyaz felt very touched.

Spontaneously, she kissed Oluwa and that sparked off sexual rage within minutes with Oluwa springing her up in his arms and taking her straight to the shower. "Let's shower together."

Niyaz went crimson, she was shy. What she did in the darkness of night once or twice with Oluwa in his apartment was not the same as living in with him for a week. Yet she surrendered. The hormones of need spiralled within her, she did not try to stop it midway. That evening would be etched in her memories forever, when Oluwa was at his best, cuddling her, bathing her, soaping her, as his lips rested on every part of her bare body, the streams from the shower engulfing them into eternal bliss.

After the shattering climax, Niyaz was super hungry. Like a child she gulped the dish Oluwa prepared and found tomato, onion, pepper in the rice meal. "What is so special about this Oluwa? It is like having rice with our curries," she teased Oluwa a bit.

"No Madam, this has special spices."

"What spices?"

"Oh! That's a secret recipe. I shall not divulge," Oluwa gave his mischievous smile as he held her hand across the table. "Nigeria has a varied and rich culinary tradition and we give a lot of importance to the aroma, we do not mix and cook veggies like you do."

"So will I recruit you as my kitchen maid?" Niyaz laughed jokingly.'

"Why not My Lady. Anything for you."

The week went off in a hush. Once or twice Naim had called to know if she was keeping well, though she never bothered to call him. Every morning, she called her mother to know if the children had been sent to school and if the driver arrived on time. Her mother Raziya bibi asked: "Come home Niyaz, why is your work needed a week? Can't you finish your meetings in 2-3 days? You belong to the house Niyaz, even if your Abbu raised you like a son, you are not a man."

Niyaz never liked these thoughts of her mother. Yet she did not protest. "Yes, Ammi I am coming soon. Do not worry."

3

After a week or so the duo were back to Dhaka and though they kept touch over calls and phone, Niyaz got busy with her work and family specially with her mother and sister staying at her house, she had to be extra careful. Her mother Raziya asked too many questions, just like any other mother, she was careful about the well being of all her daughters. With her husband dying suddenly, she was left alone, and her daughters were her prized trophies. Among them, Niyaz was however the most accomplished, but she knew she was also the most headstrong. Her father had pampered her to that extent that she would defy many social rules since her teenage years. Raziya biwi was thus very happy when she was married to Naim, who was her childhood friend and she was sure he would successfully control her emotions and they would have a great family life. Off late however, she had observed a change in her daughter's attitude. She had gone very quiet and always locked herself in her bedroom, so that none could enter without asking. Previously when Ammi came, she would sit for hours with her and speak on their village farmlands and share memories of their days with father.

This time however Raziya was surprised to find Niyaz absent-minded even at the dining table. So much so that at a point she even forgot that her seven-year-old son Abdul could not sift through the bones of Hilsa and gave it to him to eat.

"Arrey Niyaz, why are you giving that fish to Abdul. How can he eat it?" Her sister Roshanara snatched the fish from Abdul's plate, as he was about to put a large chunk with bones in his mouth. Raziya Biwi also got alarmed, but such an act seemed not to move Niyaz a bit. She kept on looking at her phone every other second. Her mother had observed that before and asked: "Do you have a meeting again? Or will Naim call from Hong Kong? Are you waiting for his call?"

Her 10-year-old daughter Soha blurted out: "Abbu calls us granny. Ammi doesn't have time to call him. So, he told me from now on he will call me to know how everyone is at home." Soha was quite proud that she was given preference by her father over her mother. But Raziya smelled a rat. She was apprehensive that all was not OK in the marriage. Else why would Naim call the children and not his wife? She also observed Niyaz was eating in silence, as if none of the words had registered her. She then left after her meal, saying a brief good bye and declaring she was so tired that she needed sleep. A worried Raziya Bibi looked at her daughter. She could sense something was wrong. But what was it?

That night Oluwa neither called, nor messaged. Niyaz kept on messaging, but no replies came. She was angry at a point. Didn't they spend a fabulous week together? And now he has just forgotten her? How convenient! At a point she even wondered: "Has anything happened to him? Is he in an accident?" She did not have any of his room mates' numbers and hence there was no way she could call and verify if all was ok with him. The only way out would be to visit him once. Well, she would do that next morning for sure.

Sleep eluded Niyaz. She kept thinking weird thoughts, drifting in and out of sleep and got up very early as the Namaz was blaring on the mic. She looked tired and she was in a rush to go out. Her mother stopped her and said: "Will you not bid your children well before leaving? What's wrong with you Niyaz. Youa re leaving even before they are going to school."

Raziya Bibi was truly surprised. "Ammi your generation will never understand how women of our generation are juggling work and family. I do not have any time trying to show them my extra love by cooking and staying with them. I am earning to make their future secure."

"Your husband also earns quite well and you know your father had left behind properties and farms for all three daughters. You are well provided and so are your children."

Seething in subtle anger, Niyaz replied: "So what you want, I shall stay in a purdah like you did all your life?"

Her Ammi was shocked. "Niyaz whatever you do, remember you have a family. A lovely and happy family. A supportive husband. You have two wonderful children. I don't know what has gone into your head, if you want to tell me, do tell. Else take reins of your life and do not make a mess!"

4

Even before her mother could end the conversation, Niyaz stormed out of the house, grabbing just an apple and skipping breakfast. Her children kept staring at their Granny. She felt so upset at Oluwa not calling or texting her, that she felt an urgent need to rush to him. Without thinking twice, she asked her driver to take a detour before going to the hospital. She parked the car in the lane opposite to the apartment where Oluwa lived and walked to the house. As she entered his flat, she heard loud laughter and music, even though the day had just begun. Thick smoke of cigarettes came through the half-opened door. Instead of knocking, she peered in and found to her dismay Oluwa sitting with his roommates and a couple of friends, she hadn't met before and making merry. They were all drunk and many empty alcohol bottles were lying on the floor. Half eaten food plates were strewn around. Some African drumbeats came from Oluwa's room. So, this is what Oluwa had been doing, enjoying himself without her! Ignoring her! Swathes of jealousy, anger, sense of loss ripped Niyaz simultaneously. She could not explain even to herself her reactions. Being a sophisticated woman, well-read, Niyaz should have left the place then and there. But the demons inside popped their heads above her conscious thoughts and Niyaz just barged in anger, shouting at Oluwa, her voice raised above the cacophony around.

"Oluwa, why didn't you call me yesterday? Who are these people? Since when have you been drinking?"

Like a sudden earthquake, the merriment around jolted a bit. A hushed silence fell, other than the African drumbeats that still kept up the show. Just like the other men around, Oluwa too could not believe his eyes. What was Niyaz doing first thing in the morning. One of his friends fumbled: "Who is this hijab beauty Bro? Your girlfriend?"

The statement made Niyaz angrier and she shouted even further: "I waited for your messages and calls all night and instead of replying you were drinking? You fraud!"

Before she could complete her sentence, Oluwa dragged her inside her room and turning the drumbeat music off, he now shouted: "So I can't drink and be happy with my friends. Is it? I always have to be with you?"

"Yes, you have to be!" Niyaz was adamant. "You have to be, why didn't you take my calls?" Even before she could speak further, in a sudden rage, Oluwa slapped Niyaz. Like a flying crane shot by an arrow, dropping dead on the ground, the slap rested for a brief second, hard and strong, Oluwa's fingers left a deep imprint on Niyaz's soft fair cheeks.

For a brief second, Niyaz just looked at him, it was difficult to fathom the multitude of emotions playing in her eyes in that split time. Without one word, Niyaz left the room and walked out of the apartment. Her steps not as strong as the ones she had when she entered. She rushed down, walked to the opposite lane, pulling her hijab closer to the spot where Oluwa had hit her. Her car was waiting at the same spot. Without a word, she opened the door and just said: "Gaffar chacha take me home."

The tears that were daring to burst out, challenging her to scream out all her frustrations, fell uncontrollably. She knew Gaffar chacha was watching her through the rear mirror. He had been with her family since her father's time and even after marriage Niyaz appointed the elderly man for her car, so that she felt safe. But today the car no more felt safe, the world had turned upside down, the man for whom she had given up partially on her children and husband and extended family, the man who she paid to go to his country and return, who she had paid for his father's treatment, had abused her! Niyaz just turned into a stone within, though the ripples of tears that inconsolably poured down her cheeks spoke of a broken heart.

Chapter 7

The Slap of Reality

1

By the time Niyaz reached home, the pitter patter tear drops had gave way to a deluge. And she did not dare look up, Chacha also did not dare ask her what was wrong. He was old enough to realise where to speak and where not to, though he had seen Niyaz as a child, but he had observed a sea change in the girl over the years. Once home, Niyaz locked herself in her room. It was just past lunch time and her mother and sister and even the maids had gone for a nap after lunch. Her children were still in school. Niyaz somewhat thanked Allah for the same, she was now in no position to face another human soul, she was so confused from within. She just needed to change, and reflect, she was now a bundle of nerves. Now was not the right time to face anyone, she was sure she was at the tether of a breakdown.

The first thing Niyaz did was to have a warm bath, even in summer. The water felt like washing away all her grime, as if she was trying to get rid of layers of her existence. Just like the streaming water, her tears also streamed down. Looking at the bathroom mirror she could clearly see a large red mark on her face, exactly the place where Oluwa had slapped her. The intensity of his strong hands was so great that it had left a mark on her tender face, not to mention the permanent jostle it had given to her heart, shattering it to pieces, like that fragile mirror that had once fallen from her hands and broke. It was a Venetian one that her husband had gifted her from one of his tours to Italy. She cried silently, she could not even howl, lest her relatives in the other room heard it. And then a thought crept into Niyaz's head. How will she conceal the mark? What will she tell her mother? She knew she was very observant and would not leave questioning her. She now started thinking what story she would make up. As she wrapped the towel around her, she dreamt of the day when Oluwa had first touched her, that was so tender, despite his large and strong frame, every finger of his caressing her skin. But as the wave of that long-lost moment lingered, she shuddered to think how that tender touch had suddenly gave way to an abusive slap! Niyaz cringed in fear.

Lying on her bed, with the room AC in full blast, Niyaz just stay still. The world around her seemed to have halted, was she living in a bubble for so many months, and now that she got stuck to the harsh reality, what will she do? The dilemma ate her up, made her vulnerable. Only if Naim was here right then, to take her into his reassuring embrace? Was she being cruel to Naim? Well, it was she who left him for another man? As all these conflicting thoughts barged through her senses, Niyaz drifted to sleep. She was tired, sleep was her haven of solitary bliss. As she was floating in an abyss of darkness, a rude knock brought her back to the world of humans. She got up. Someone was knocking at the door. It was Ammi.

"Niyaz, when did you arrive? Are you sleeping? Your children have come from school. Open the door, they need to use the toilet."

Niyaz jumped out of bed, snatched the hijab lying on the chair and wore it instantly covering the red mark on her face. She quickly opened the door. Her son bounced in, almost knocking her off balance, he was always so full of energy. He clasped Niyaz's legs and said: "Oh Ammi, am so happy you are already home. Shall we play today after snacks?"

He hardly ever got his mother close, and with the absence of his father most of the time, he being the youngest in the family always vied for Niyaz's attention. Niyaz just nodded and asked him to take a bath as the maid walked in with his home clothes. Raziya Bibi was an observant woman, instantly she realized something was wrong with her daughter. Why was she wearing a hijab at home? Niyaz never wore one at home. She had started wearing one outside as Naim's family had been conservative and did not want the woman of the house to go out on work. Though he convinced them that she had to go, for he would not confine an educated woman behind closed doors, then they gave a diktat, in that case she had to wear a hijab. Raziya Bibi had thus convinced Niyaz to compromise for deep down she knew Naim was the best match for her fiery and stubborn child.

2

Today she again realized something was amiss. "Niyaz are you unwell?" she enquired.

"No," Niyaz said softly.

"Then why did you return so early? Did you have lunch? I heard from Gaffar that you did not go to the hospital?"

"Yes, I had work outside," Niyaz spoke in self-defence. "Why do I need to tell everyone where I am going?"

Well, that was a defiant answer for sure and Raziya understood all was not well. And suddenly the hijab shifted a bit, as Niyaz was hurriedly shifting through the plates on the dining table as if to lay the table for her children to have their snacks, she saw the red mark. Instinctively like any mother, she removed the hijab and was shocked to see the mark. She knew it was a mark of hurt.

"Oh Allah, where did you hurt yourself."

In a desperate attempt to cover it up, Niyaz tried to pull the hijab back again. Raziya was adamant: "Niyaz, look at me, you never wear a hijab at home. What are you trying to cover?"

"Nothing Ammi, I got hurt when I walked in on the door panel. I did not wake any of you up. I shall out some ice later and it will go away."

"Look into my eyes, Niyaz, you are lying to me, why else you have your face down. Since childhood among my three daughters, you were the trouble maker always. Confess to me Niyaz what happened."

Niyaz now retaliated. She raised her voice a bit, "Nothing happened Ammi. I am a grown-up woman now with two children. Stop meddling in my life."

She knew this one sentence would hurt her Ammi, but that was the only way she could silence her from further questioning.

"OK Niyaz, I shall not ask you anymore. But take it from your Ammi, you are a married woman now with children and your husband is very supportive. You are a lucky woman for sure. Do not spoil your life by doing something foolish."

Niyaz did not reply. She got busy working with her maid to lay the afternoon snacks for her children, a task she had hardly done since the time she met Oluwa and spent almost every evening with him or in his thoughts. After months it seemed she found the old rhythm of life again. That night she called Naim and he was surprised too. There was a hint of sarcasm in his tone: "Oh my my, Niyaz, so what's up today. I am a lucky man as to receive your call."

Niyaz brushed aside his sarcasm and asked simple questions: "How is your work going? When are you coming next? Any new business connects?" And so on.

But Naim was not ready to be bowled over by the sweet tone in her voice. For months he felt neglected, as if Niyaz was more into other people and ignoring him. So, he kept saying: "Good that you suddenly woke up from your delirium and wishing to know about my business. So, are you giving up your hospital and joining me?"

As Niyaz kept quiet to his sarcasm, Naim softened a bit. "How are my children? They were asking me the other day when I shall return. I told them Ammi would bring them to me in London and we shall all visit Switzerland. They will love the castles and dairy farms."

Niyaz just said a meek OK, bid him good night. Somehow, she felt sane and comfortable after speaking to Naim. She knew him since childhood, their teenage years were spent in fun at their family homes. This man stood by all her wishes, trying to compromise at every step. How could she ignore the love he gave him. Maybe he was unable to satisfy her always sexually, maybe he stayed away on work for months, maybe he was not poetic or could not do the sweet talk that made her feel important and happy, yet he was dedicated to the kids and family for sure. That night Niyaz spoke to herself: "I should have been more kind to Naim. Allah, please forgive me for my *gunaah*. I was out of my mind."

3

The next morning came with a new promise. Niyaz tried convincing herself not to even open the barrage of messages that kept coming from Oluwa, not to mention the multiple calls that landed over phone. She just convinced herself that a man who had the guts to hit her, should not be entertained at any cost. She had never been hit by any man before, not even by her father when they were children. Niyaz was always a very energetic and naughty child and though her mother scolded or even pulled her hair and slapped her at times, she never got a scolding from her father. She was his queen. Naim too was never abusive, even when he ever got angry. He would go quiet and stop talking and eating but never raised his hand on her. The poison of insult that inflicted her heart was too much to bear. Niyaz had to forget all the moments spent with Oluwa to shake off the insult.

Entering her hospital, she called her assistant and gave strict instructions: "Do not allow anyone to enter my room. I am busy, if anyone tries to barge in, throw him or her out."

Niyaz's assistant was quite taken aback by her senior's aggressive tone. She just nodded and left. Soon Oluwa arrived, something Niyaz had anticipated. He kept on insisting that the meeting was a must. The assistant however was hell bent not to let him in. He still kept pestering: "Tell your maam, please, that it is Oluwa. I shall only take 5 minutes. It is about some reports."

"Please go to the front desk and ask them." The assistant replied.

"No, I need to talk to her."

"She is busy Sir and will not meet anyone today."

Meanwhile, Oluwa saw a doctor enter the room. A guard was standing by the door. On previous occasions he had never seen a guard before. Oluwa still did not lose hope. After waiting for half an hour, he again went to the assistant and said: "The front desk could not help maam. Can you please at least call up your madam and tell her I wish to speak on phone."

"No, we cannot do that Sir. We have our own rules."

Oluwa realized, this way there was no chance of any meeting and too much persuasion might cause more harm than intended. So, he left that day. But he kept on with his messages and calls constantly. Almost a week passed and Niyaz did not reply, nor did she meet. Meanwhile, Niyaz drowned herself into work, expansion of business, meetings with medical professionals and started giving more time to home. She took her children and mother and sister shopping over the weekend and treated them to dinner. Their smiling faces were posted on Instagram and Naim also commented. In fact, he called her almost every evening, and kept saying how beautiful London and Europe in general was and how he got a client from Hong Kong who also had an office in UK. They would be soon signing a business agreement. "I thought I should break the good news to you first Niyaz." Naim sounded happy.

Niyaz kept up the show. Though the red mark on her face faded with the passing days, the deep hurt it had left on the heart was still staring bare like a raw wound, waiting to be mended.

4

In the beginning of the week next, Niyaz had an unusual visitor at her chamber. Since Oluwa was no more showing up, Niyaz had asked her assistant not to stop other visitors from coming over if they asked for a meeting with her. That Monday, Niyaz was sitting in her chamber, a bit absent-minded. It had been over a week, that she thought she had successfully dissociated from the 'Oluwa charm' that had possessed her for months. Still, his face kept hovering on the chair that stood empty by her. The first day he had entered her room, that man of tall and broad frame, walking with a limp. The day he kissed her first in that same chamber and literally took her breath away. The more Niyaz tried to drive away the thoughts of Oluwa crowding her head, they kept creeping in so much so that she opened a couple of files to go through them. She needed distraction, just like last week when she was with work or family, deeply involved.

Just as she was turning the pages of one file, she saw a man walking in, after a small knock. For a second, her heart skipped. Is it Oluwa? The same dark skin, but shorter frame of a man, sat infront. Oh! It was Obike, his cousin. "What are you doing here? Who has sent you? Why have you come?"

Obike quite obligingly replied: "Sorry maam, I am bothering you…."

Even before he could finish his sentence relating the purpose of his visit, Niyaz said: "If you need any medical related issue to be solved, please go to the front desk, didn't my assistant tell you that?" Niyaz sounded irritated.

"Maam, please maam, hear me out. Oluwa wishes to tell you everything of his past life, please bear with him and meet him one last time. I told you he has many secrets. Now he wishes to confess."

"Why confess to me, Obike?"

"Oh! because he loves you and says he wants to do penance by telling you everything."

"Oh really? And that's why he slapped me?"

"He is very repentant for that, madam. He was dead drunk that day and you came in without informing. We were not prepared."

"So, he can slap? Huh! You support physical abuse."

"No maam, it happened in the spur of the moment, it was a big mistake for sure, please hear him out, give him one chance. I am requesting you on behalf of Oluwa."

Niyaz was a bit disturbed, all these months she was anyway keen to know what Oluwa was up to and all about his past life. Now that he was giving her the chance, she should take it one last time. She said: "Ok, on Wednesday I shall meet him at the coffee shop where we first met and ask him to come around 3pm. The coffee shop is usually empty during that time. I do not wish to create a scene before anyone. Who know what he is up to now?"

"No no maam, do not get him wrong, he is a very well-mannered man, the slap was unintended. I assure you, he is a kind hearted man.

Niyaz kept silent. She was not ready to make any decision about Oluwa's character. His actions had already confused him to a large extent. Obike kept saying: "I shall let him know about the time and date. Thank you maam for hearing me out. Will not bother you anymore."
Saying so Obike bid a good bye.

On Wednesday, Niyaz literally dragged herself to the hospital. Something within was throwing her into a whirlpool of conflicting thoughts. "Why was she going? What did she intend to find out?" Still, something pulled her towards that coffee shop. She kept telling herself: "This would be one last time."

Before she walked through the gates, she could see Oluwa waiting in the designated seat where they first sat. Seeing her enter, he got up quickly and came forward to shake hands. However, Niyaz refused to give her hands and sat down quietly. He immediately brought out a red rose from a packet he was carrying and offered it to Niyaz: "This is for you. Please forgive me. I am a sinner. You are my dainty princess, how could I behave like a demon and hit you? Punish me any way you wish to, I shall accept it. If you want, slap me back in public!"

Niyaz still kept quiet, she was not a woman to give in so easily, specially after abuse. Her resilience against any male abuse had made her so independent for all these years. And here was a man, rather a stranger, who hit her and still she agreed to meet him one last time.

In a matter-of-fact tone, she said: "Obike told me, you wished to speak about your past life, I have no time discussing anything else."

"Yes, yes My Lady, he was correct. I wish to download all the sorrow that have been bothering me for years. You are the woman I love, and I shall no more hold back anything."

And thus, Oluwa started narrating the tales of his life, with Niyaz listening intently. The café was empty, barring a college couple at the far end, gossiping, holding hands.

Chapter 8

Tales of Betrayal

1

Oluwa was a budding footballer, struggling to make a name, when he met the woman of his life, he fell in love head over heels, only to be betrayed. One day after returning from his club practice, he found, Abe was nowhere around and their little boy, was sitting on the courtyard and crying. He rushed in, all his youthful charm vanishing, seeing his crying baby, he enquired from his mother-in-law who was washing clothes in the courtyard about the whereabouts of Abe.

"Where is she?"

"Abe has gone somewhere, may be to the market."

Oluwa picked up their baby and walked to the front entrance only to see a car parked in the distance. To his utter dismay he found Abe in the car kissing his friend Abraham, the guy who stayed next door and also played football with him. Abraham was clutching Abe's breasts and sucking them, Abe's dress had dipped low, and she was laughing and enjoying the act. Feeling disgusted and betrayed, Oluwa had walked into his house until almost an hour later, he found Abe sneaking through the back gate. When he confronted her about her alleged affair, she started blackmailing him, threatening to kill herself. She also practiced black magic on him. This was the time when Oluwa met his present Nigerian wife at the church. She was an outspoken lady and through her spiritual powers, she healed him. They became friends and Oluwa felt largely indebted to her for saving her from the clutches of a disdainful Abe.

He started living in with her and they had their first boy together. Though they had not married yet, they were surely thinking of a life together. Meanwhile, Oluwa got an offer from an Indian club in Goa. Once in India, Oluwa's football career took off and he started playing in different Goan clubs and earning loads of money. He started sending most of the money back home to support his two sons, one with Abe and the other with his present wife. But life of a footballer is like a gypsy. He played from club to club and kept shifting from place to place. While staying in a beachside house, he met the Goan beauty Alvita.

2

Alvita was his house-owner's daughter. She was dainty, beautiful, fragile. Oluwa was then not married to his present wife and they just had a child. He also wanted to get an Indian citizenship, so that he would no more be on a work visa as a footballer and could explore more opportunities in other parts of India. He even called his fiancée in Nigeria and she agreed that Oluwa could marry Alvita and get a permanent residency in India that would help his career to grow. After all, without a formal higher education, Oluwa had to play to survive or do some business in India that would help him send money back home.

But Alvita had many demands. She was not ready to accept the fact that Oluwa would travel between Nigeria and India often, when not playing in the clubs. She did not wish Oluwa to keep any relation with his Nigerian fiancée or even with his family. That was impossible for Oluwa to accept as he had two sons from two women, he had his father still alive and ailing and also his brother and sisters who loved and cared for him. How could he abandon his own family and be dedicated to Alvita! But Alvita and her father refused to listen to Oluwa's sighs and thus the possible marriage broke even before it could materialize. So Oluwa returned to Nigeria during the lean soccer season, with a mind to be back to India soon.

Once in Nigeria, he started staying with Myaka, his fiancée, who had a bit of good spiritual influence on him. He loved his son beyond imagination, very attached to him and also sent money for his first born to Abe for his studies. Myaka and Oluwa decided to tie the knot in a complete traditional church marriage. Marital bliss followed and Myaka got pregnant with their second child. Time was running out and so was money. Oluwa had to start his stint as a footballer again to earn. He applied for many clubs and the jackpot was won when he was recruited by a Kolkata club. He again travelled to India from Nigeria, this time with a longer stint to stay and earn enough to support his large family. Not just his own sons, and the newborn arriving soon, Oluwa also had his younger sister's children to support. His sister Fulake's husband left for another woman and thus she was alone with her two daughters. She was working hard to meet both ends and Oluwa paid for the children's education. His younger brother had left the family long back and was very well off, working in a bank in the capital Lagos. Though he at times visited their father and gave him some money, but that was not regular. His elder sister was also working in the city as a real estate agent, but did not bother much about Oluwa or his large family that he had to support all by himself.

3

Once in India and playing in Kolkata's clubs, springing from one to the other, running along the goalposts, practicing on the Maidan, Oluwa realized for the first time that his knees were giving away. That vital part of a footballer's body on which his core strength stands. Oluwa realized his career in soccer would soon be over and he had to make the best use of his time and strength while in Kolkata. Myaka by then had given birth to their second baby boy and he needed to send more money home. So, he and his wife decided to start a garments business in a small way at Nigeria from their grocery shop. Kolkata had cheap markets where one got a variety of fabrics that could be traded in and thus, he started exporting them. Myaka also advised him to try and get an Indian citizenship that would help in trading better.

Oluwa told many of his friends about getting into a contractual marriage and getting hold of an Indian citizenship in the process. Oluwa had a natural charm and all his life he had observed women easily fell for him, may be his kind eyes did the trick. Other than a multitude of call girls and prostitutes, who he picked from the hotels and night clubs of Kolkata, Oluwa had a bevy of beauties falling for him. His Nigerian friend Adam who also played in a small soccer club of Kolkata one day brought a match for him - an Anglo-Indian woman named Leeanna Jordan who was a divorcee with a son. She worked as an office assistant and needed a house to stay and money to support her son's education. She agreed to a contractual marriage that would be mutually beneficial. Leeanna would get a place to stay with her son and money to support the family, while Oluwa stood a chance to gain an Indian citizenship. Myaka also agreed to the terms and she and Leeanna even met on a video call between two continents. They were happy and struck a great friendship.

Oluwa took a flat in the Picnic Garden area and they started living together after a proper church marriage attended by almost 200 guests. Leeanna and Oluwa were in the beginning strict about the rules of live in as they had decided they would not have any sexual relationship. He slept with Leeanna's son in one bedroom while Leeanna slept in the other. But she never failed to wear seductive dresses when Oluwa was around and even entice him over a drink. However, Oluwa had no intention to have any sexual contact with her. He was happy with the prostitutes, he would drop in at their quarters often after a match. He had also been to a local hospital and taken contraceptive injections as he had no intention to use a condom or to make another woman pregnant. He already had a string of offsprings and was in no position to support another.

4

But all did not go as per plan. One rainy evening as Oluwa sat for a drink, Leeanna joined. She was wearing a spaghetti top, with her big breasts bulging out inviting any man to get a touch of the same. She had deliberately sent her son that evening to her mother's place and it being a weekend, he would not return before Monday morning after school. Oluwa after a few drinks could no more control his sex urge and Leeanna was provocative enough to enjoy with him. They started touching each other, and the urge grew so high that they literally tore their clothes and made it out on the sofa. Little did Oluwa realise this would soon be a habit and quite often Oluwa and Leeanna started having sex. After a few months, Leeanna came in with a report saying she was pregnant. Oluwa was shocked, for he knew he was taking contraceptive injections and it was next to impossible that she could get pregnant.

He also knew she was having sex with his friend David and it might be his child too. But Oluwa was very clear that Leeanna needed to abort the child as he was not ready to be a father again. Leeanna demanded around 30,000 from Oluwa and he was forced to pay for the abortion. But Leeanna atleast stuck to her words and had the abortion done. As the days went by, she and Oluwa went out with Leeanna's extended family of brothers, sisters and mother. Oluwa loved her son a lot and promised to support him always. The time came for him to return once to Nigeria and Leeanna agreed he should go back for a few months and take as much garments he could from India and Bangladesh and make brisk business in Lagos and other smaller towns of Nigeria. By then Oluwa had also earned enough from the soccer clubs and once he reached Nigeria, he built a house for Myaka and the children. He and the children had loads of fun, for Oluwa this was home and now that he had money, it was great to provide everyone with even gifts that they wished for months. Myaka also tried hard to set up their garments business from their small shop and they were selling well. Meanwhile she again became pregnant and being a Christian, it was against their faith to abort the child. So Myaka kept the baby. Oluwa would be a father again.

After a couple of months, it was time for Oluwa to return to India and start earning again, partly from soccer, but mainly from his business. He called up Leeanna and informed, he would come soon and gave her the date. And thus started his return journey to India, a chapter of his life that would play with his fate and change it forever.

As Oluwa kept narrating one tale after the other, Niyaz wondered if this was his real life or was he making up some stories atleast. The trust factor that Niyaz had on this man had vanished from her soul and she no longer felt that she should believe whatever Oluwa was telling her.

She retorted: "Why didn't you talk about all this before? And if you did not, why are you saying now?"

Oluwa looked quite distraught. "Believe me My Lady I did not wish to disturb you with my life tales. But because you no more believe me, I thought of keeping no part of my life hidden. I want to tell you all."

Niyaz felt quite uncomfortable, a raging storm in her heart. To believe, or not to believe --- that was the uppermost question now.

Chapter 9

A House of Lies

1

As Oluwa landed at Netaji Subhash Chandra airport from Dubai, Leeanna was waiting for him at the lounge. She would be meeting him after quite a number of months and was wearing a lovely dress to entice him. At a point Leeanna apprehended that Oluwa would forget her after reaching Nigeria and meeting his family. Thankfully he didn't. Seeing Oluwa coming out through the exit gate, Leeanna rushed to him and hugged him tight. But as soon as she did, a group of armed policemen suddenly appeared and arrested Oluwa as well as Leeanna. A bit of commotion ensued, with onlookers around trying to fathom what had occurred and with a shocked Oluwa shouting at times in English and at times in his native language with a look of disbelief. As for Leeanna, she was howling and demanding from the police why they were being arrested. However, the police force had their cars waiting outside and without creating much of a scene, forced the duo to enter the standing vehicle.

They were taken to the police station.

Oluwa kept asking: "Why did you arrest me?"

Meanwhile, the police started searching the bags Oluwa was carrying and they dug out his Nigerian passport along with a series of credit cards and punching machines with duplicate pins. The police seized them and asked them authoritatively: "Where are you staying now?"

Oluwa refused to reply but Leeanna gave the police their Picnic Garden address out of fear. The police had their own tactics to squeeze out information and they went all out on this couple. They already had reasons to track them down. When some of their officials reached their house, they went through all the documents and stacks of papers in the cupboard. Leeanna's son was with his grandmother now as the police had sealed Leeanna's flat. While the search was one, a constable suddenly felt a closed chamber in the back of one cupboard. A carpenter was called to open the lock of the secret chamber and out poured a series of more machines and international credit cards as also swipe machines. They found several gold jewellery and expensive watches. With all these in hand, the police took the duo in custody.

When Leeanna's mother reached the police station with a lawyer, she literally broke down. She asked the officer in charge: "Sir, please let me know what my daughter has done. She is a good girl. We have been residing in this city for ages. She can never be part of any fraud gang. I have no idea about that Nigerian guy. Please release my daughter."

When the lawyer asked as to which sections were given for the arrest and what was the reason for the arrest, the investigating officer said in clear words: "We received at least five different complaints from customers of a leading bank who use international credit cards and stay in different parts of the world. They complained that huge amounts of transactions amounting to almost 50 lakhs were done from their cards, though they never used these cards ever. The case came to the city Police Headquarters and while investigating, the investigating officers came across the name of Oluwa. The investigating officer Sanjay Kumar said: "This is an international racket involving at least 3 Nigerians and 2 Indians. Oluwa is one of them. He has a Nigerian

counterpart in Canada who used to make these fake credit cards and through some means, got hold of the pins and sent them to Oluwa and the other Nigerian guy. They would then use these cards to carry out lakhs of transactions from various places, usually they bought gold and other expensive items and later sell them off against cash."
Leeanna's mother still crying asked: "But what did my daughter do? Why did you arrest her? Please believe me she had no hand in this."

The inspector mockingly laughed at the old lady and said: "Maam, please go home." Then turning to the lawyer, he said: "You know in such cases you have to apply for bail. But we too have to investigate if somehow your client is also a part of this racket, though we have got names of other accomplices like Adams and Nigel. The hunt is on for them too and they will soon be rounded off."

2

It was a few months ago that the head of the bank's Risk Containment Unit (RCU, the division that attempts to keep transactions between the bank and its customers as risk-free as possible) had a call with Kolkata Police Headquarters. He was relating a fraud, his voice extremely tense and distraught.

"Officer, we are at a total loss. What shall we do? The losses on these fraudulent credit cards have now gone past 20 lakhs. Head office is mailing or calling every day. It's driving us insane. At first, we thought it was a technical problem, which we could sort out internally, but that hasn't happened, we now realised there is a big fraud racket behind these dubious transactions. Please do something, sir. Our bank's reputation is at stake."

The police officer on the other side of the phone asked for details and got to know that details of ATM cards belonging to various customers of different banks are somehow being accessed by a group of crooks. The bank head related how the fraud happens. "Say Ram keeps his money in a bank in America, which has issued a credit card. All information related to that card is then stolen, and transferred to a card in this country, belonging to say Shyam. Which essentially means that Shyam can now use Ram's card to go on a spending spree. The same is happening between Jadu and Madhu. The moment Ram and Jadu learn that their money have vanished, they naturally approach their banks, furious at their loss, demanding compensation for they hadn't spent anything. What can the American bank do but collate all the evidence and write to the Indian bank which has issued the credit card, demanding their customers' rightful money back. The bank has no option but to pay up. And so, our losses keep mounting Sir."

"Is it your bank only that is hard hit?" The officer's tone sounded very serious.

"Yes sir, the bank here has been particularly hurt by this scam, and it is rapidly spiralling out of control. The losses are now countable in lakhs rather than thousands, and will soon cross into crores."

"What did your bank find after the internal enquiry?"

"That's ongoing, sir. But we haven't really made progress. Something happened the day before yesterday, though."

"What?" The officer sounded very interested.

"We had alerted each of our EDCs (electronic data counters). A young man bought quite an expensive gold chain from a shop in Bowbazar and paid with a credit card. The staff were a little suspicious of the card and asked for some ID. And he provided a driving licence, bearing a blurred imprint of a face. We got this verified, sir, from Motor Vehicles. It's a fake driving license."

"Whose license is it?"

"The name on the licence reads Mohammed Sikander," the bank officer stated.

"Fine. Submit a written complaint at the local thana. Let a case be registered and then we shall start the investigation."

That night, the investigative officer, Sanjay was called in. When briefed, he realised this was a case of 'Card Skimming.' These two words are now familiar to many. It's been barely a month since an ATM fraud scare swept through Kolkata. Plenty of people lost money. The kingpins of the racket were a few Romanian citizens, whose very swift capture from different parts of the country thankfully prevented further loss of many more people's hard- earned money.

Sanjay realised this scam had to be resolved quickly, as a scam as big as this, could potentially weaken the entire banking system. Ordinary people stand to lose money. This particular flower needs to be nipped in the bud. However, the hunt for a criminal can only begin once the how and why and when of a crime is known. Trawling the internet, reading up as much as he could, Sanjay made every effort to explain it to his colleagues. He had already formed a team of cyber crime experts. At the team meeting he explained: "The brown band on the reverse of a credit or debit card is the repository of quite a lot of invisible, confidential information. Which is not accessible even by bank staff. Say someone steals that information and, using technology to extrapolate that information onto the brown band on another card, uses the second card. This, in short, is skimming."

One of Sanjay's team member Atul asked: "But how does the theft happen?"

"Say, you are at an ATM counter. You insert your card in the green slot beneath the computer screen as you always do. You don't have the foggiest idea that the green slot has a machine (skimming device) fitted to it, which instantly records all the information stored in your card. You then use the keypad to punch in your secret PIN number, once again without realising that yet another keypad fitted perfectly over the original records your PIN number too. Once you leave the ATM, the rest is childishly simple for the scammers, who detach the skimming device which they had installed earlier. They use the stolen information to create dummy cards and steal other people's money."

And this was an international scam, hence frightfully big amounts were being skimmed off. The bank officer had explained to him the figures. "Say the value of the Indian rupee against the American dollar is 70 to 1. Now imagine someone steals an American customer's card details. Those details make their way to an accomplice in India, who is already in possession of an Indian card, delivered to a false address. This card shows a balance of zero. The accomplice then walks into a jewellery outlet, for instance, and buys jewellery worth 100 dollars, or Rs 7,000. The American customer's card shows a transaction of 100 dollars, and the thief vanishes with the jewellery. The shop owner has no idea that he has just sold jewellery to a buyer who is using someone else's card details. Rather, he collects the 'charge slip' generated during the sale, deposits it at the bank the next day, and picks up Rs 7,000."

Another team member asked Sanjay: "Then when does everyone wake up?"

"When the American customer raises hell at his bank. He hadn't purchased, not just that, he was in no way in India! And someone transacted in India with his card and pin. So, the American bank now asks the Indian bank for 100 dollars, backed by irrefutable evidence. The Indian bank is forced to reimburse the American bank from its own exchequer. The purchase details against the card were in order. Simply, the American card holder's information was stolen and fed into the Indian card."

3

The investigative team had indeed a very difficult job in hand. The crime followed no known patterns, the source network was of no use. The only concrete piece of information was the photocopy of the fake driving license, with its blurred image. Sanjay made it a point to inform all the police stations across the city and put them on high alert. Information was shared with those commercial establishments in every area where card transactions were done. They were asked to stay alert, too, and let the police know the moment they spot anything unusual to do with any such transaction. About ten days after the case was registered by the bank, the first bit of news came to one of the city police station.

Two young men had walked into an electronic gadgets' shop to buy a laptop, using a card. Once the card was swiped, however, a discrepancy was detected between the card number and the print slip. One of the men was made to wait at the shop, while the other went to fetch another card. As soon as the Bank Fraud section heard of this, Sanjay and his team rushed to the spot. They rounded off one man named Ankan Tewari, but the other man who was supposedly coming back with the card seemed to have vanished into thin air.

Who was the mystery man? After a nightlong question-answer session at the police headquarters, Ankan revealed that he did not know his companion all that long. His name was Manimay Agarwal, and the two met at a tea shop on Middleton Street. A few days ago, he had asked Ankan for help in buying a laptop. "You're tech savvy, I've decided to buy a laptop, can you come along? Just to explain the specifications, so I don't end up buying the wrong thing."

The police asked Ankan about Manimay's whereabouts and got to know he lived near Alipore. But he could not give them any definite address, or a mobile number as Ankan said he does not have his mobile number.

Sanjay got frustrated at this. He banged the table infront of Ankan and said harshly: "What do you mean, you don't have the number?"

"Really sir, I don't. I don't have a mobile myself, and never really needed his number. I hadn't known him that long."

The only silver lining to emerge from the entire exercise was when Ankan was shown the photograph of Mohammed Sikandar as found on the driving license, he said: "Oh here is Manimay." Ankan was released as Sanjay and his team wanted to use him as a pawn to nab the actual culprit. Ankan had no idea that two officers in plain clothes were following him silently, at a safe distance. Ankan lived in Maniktala, but instead of boarding a bus home, he took a minibus headed for South Kolkata. The police in plain clothes also boarded the same bus.

Ankan got off at Park Circus, and walked a little distance to a popular coffee shop opposite Ice Skating Ring. Emerging five minutes later, he walked back to Park Circus, and this time, boarded a northbound bus. The police spoke to a service boy at the coffee shop. Surprisingly, Ankan had ordered nothing, merely said: "My name is Ankan, I was supposed to meet my friend here for coffee, but something important has come up and I have to go to the police. Some stuff was stolen from my house a few days ago and a case was filed, so the police have called me to the police headquarters. I can't stay. If anyone asks for me, tell them I'm not coming back today."

The officers also learnt that Ankan came to this shop before, once or twice a month for coffee, sometimes alone, else with friends, one of whom was a six-foot plus Nigerian who the others call Benson. He's mostly in a football jersey and shorts, and the service boy has learnt from snatches of conversation that Benson is a footballer who plays for some Maidan club. Ankan proved to be very crafty. Since the day of his questioning, he barely left his home or neighbourhood. The fact that he did not carry a mobile phone made it impossible to track who he was trying to contact. The police thus for days could not trace anything. Meanwhile, it seemed, Manimay AKA Mohammed Sikander had disappeared. The service boy at the coffee shop, also identified his photo, and volunteered the information that Manimay had told him about some close relative in Mullick Bazar, who owns a clothing store, and from whom he would help get new clothes for the boy at a discount before Chhat Puja.

There are hundreds of clothing stores in Mullick Bazar, and it was like searching for a needle in haystack. But Sanjay's team decided to set up surveillance at Mullick Bazar. But where was Benson, the Nigerian footballer? He needed to be located swiftly, and his coordinates determined. He was the only foreign connect at the moment.

His details were vital. The team was thus sent to all the known clubs of Maidan and finally a photograph of Benson was found. But it was very unclear, though the address given was YMCA Hostel, Dharamtala.

They got to know from a few fellow footballers that this guy frequented a flat on Picnic Garden for he had called them for dinner once at that location. The owner of the flat was Leeanna, an Anglo-Indian woman in her mid-30s. Attractive, divorced, mother of a boy. She worked as a receptionist in the office of a steel company on Ballygunge Circular Road. Apart from Benson, a couple of other young Nigerian men are occasional visitors there and they stay a day or two, and leave. However, there's a middle-aged Nigerian who visits about once every two months, and stays at least a fortnight. Not just a couple of days.

And that's how Oluwa and Leeanna got into the web, a web of lies that they themselves had woven, one knowingly and the other unknowingly, caught in that web. Ankush Manimay and Leeanna had turned state witnesses by submitting detailed judicial confessions. They said in a joint statement: We were used by Oluwa and his gang as pawns and we had no idea what was going behind-the-scenes. Leeanna infact mentioned to the police how she met Oluwa and how they started staying together, completely oblivious of the fact that Oluwa was linked to some fraud racket. She told Sanjay: "Sir, believe me, I just knew he is a footballer. I needed money to raise my son and thought he would pay for my son's educational expenses. I do a small job and cannot meet two ends. My husband had abandoned me long ago. I even look after my ailing mother. I had no clue that Oluwa was hoarding pins, cards and machines inside the cupboard. I never used that cupboard in my son's room, it was always kept locked by Oluwa and he had his things in it."

4

Not that Sanjay believed in Leeanna completely, but to make the case strong, he needed witnesses and who could be a better witness than Leeanna herself! Meanwhile, Oluwa also gave names of two more Nigerians who lived in USA and were part of the international racket. They would supply him with the card details using which Oluwa would make lakhs of rupees disappear sitting in Kolkata. The booty was then divided online. Sanjay realised he had to send all these details to FBI in USA to nab those in that country.

The complete trial process lasted for three years. Leeanna, Ankush and Manimay were released on bail. The three masterminds including Oluwa got a jail term for 10 years.

As Oluwa kept on relating the story, Niyaz sat like a stone. She did not even realise that the sun had set by then and as evening came, some more customers had entered the café and some of them were looking their way, specially seeing a woman in hijab having coffee with a Nigerian man. They were curious. Niyaz on the other hand could not feel any emotions. She did not know how to react. The man she had believed without a word was actually a convict and a fraud! How could she be such a fool as to believe him and even have sex with him, how could she give him money over and over. Why did not she question him whenever he spoke of returning home and asked for money? Ripped by a multitude of emotions, Niyaz felt the entire Oluwa episode of her life must have been a bad dream!

Chapter 10

The Price of Obsession

1

The high walls of the prison could not crush Oluwa. It seemed he was waiting for such a life and was ready to embrace it. In the first few months, he could not understand the ways, specially he had a language barrier as most of the prisoners spoke the local language. One day he got into a major fist fight with an Indian prisoner who called him names. Till then, he would usually keep to himself and laid in one corner of the cell and came out only when asked to for meals and work. But on that fateful Friday, the man named Kishen, kicked him as he was lying alone. He was completely unprovoked, yet he did it. Oluwa turned and looked at him sternly. Yet Kishen was not deterred, he kicked him again, this time on his penis. Oluwa was enraged and his family knew when in rage he could kill someone.

Oluwa got up and started raining blows on the man so badly that the other prisoners shouted for the jail officers who finally came and rescued Kishen from Oluwa's clutches. It was like a gladiator game of ancient Greece, Oluwa the powerful one ripping Kishen apart and the other prisoners shouting, some in glee and some in apprehension that Kishen would be killed.

The jail officials were aghast at the force with which Oluwa was hitting the man. He definitely was well-built, but for all these months he had been quiet and lived alone, not bothering others. But now he came off in his true avatar. The jail officials reprimanded him a lot, even threatening to put more sentence on him but Oluwa gave a wide grin. That was the day Oluwa realised he had to show his strength in the prison, else he would be bullied and butchered.

That's how Oluwa became the residing don, usurping the throne from Patrick. Patrick was a German prisoner who had been put behind the bars for a series of fraud a few years ago. The local and native prisoners used to worship Patrick as he looked like a demi God and was also educated. He did not fight much but he earned the respect by helping other prisoners. But now it seemed Oluwa with all his might would protect those who would join him and desert Patrick. One petty prisoner told the other: "Our new *neta* has arrived. Shun that white man now. I am telling you this man is very strong, he will protect us from bullies, if we join him."

2

Since that day a new don was born in prison. Years passed, Oluwa never got bail. Rather charges were framed against him as the state witnesses gave their testimony in court and thus Oluwa got 10 years of rigorous imprisonment. Oluwa thus realised the jail would be his home for the next many years and he had to survive in that hell hole in his own format. He thus turned a new leaf, no more the Oluwa who was soft and well mannered, who duped people with his sweet talks, who was a decent footballer, who loved to cook. He rather became the ultimate leader for the prisoners, abusing his strength and power to run a parallel drug racket from within the prison with the help of some men in uniform.

Not just that to prove his power and make others submit to him, he would rag any newly sentenced convict who was sent to prison. Everyone had to pay him *hafta* every week and he would collect that money to buy things from the prison's market. Though he hardly had visitors, most jail inmates did and their relatives would come and hand over some money weekly to them. Half of which had to be given to Oluwa as 'protection fees.' Those who did not give, Oluwa would make their life a hell. Some of his friend inmates even massaged him daily, helped with his work and did whatever he wished.

Every week he would cook once with the money he got from everyone as Oluwa was a good cook. He even sent some of his cooked meals for the lady jailer Tamasha, who took an uncanny liking to this man. The prison had Africans, Russians, rural boys, many of who were serving a long sentence. Everyone more or less belonged to the Oluwa brigade, those who didn't would be beaten and abused regularly till they submitted. But why were all inmates so kind to Oluwa? Well, that was simple, because Oluwa got into a sexual relationship with Tamasha, the lady jailer. One day, she even called him to her quarters and Oluwa gave her the best sexual experience. Since then, she would often call him and he started satisfying her in bed. Instead, he got tremendous favours and enjoyed an unwritten power over others. Every jail officer also started favouring him and the jailer gave him a cell phone which he could even use to make international calls from the jail itself. Tamasha one day said: "Hey Oluwa I know you are running a drug peddling racket from within the prison. If I ever catch you red-handed, I shall beat you black and blue."

Oluwa kissed her and then picked her on his lap, thrusting his penis into her uniform. As Tamasha melted in his arms, he said: "I will give 25 percent of the money I earn to your jail gang. I can even make it 50 percent if you want. The rest I shall send home, as you know I have my wife and children back in Nigeria." The jailer was so addicted to the wild sex that Oluwa gave her, that she accepted all his terms. Only when some higher official visited, Oluwa would be treated as any other prisoner and during inspection his phone would be hidden somewhere. Tamasha and her constables were literally hand-in-glove with the prisoner gang led by Oluwa.

3

Leeanna came one day to visit Oluwa in jail and said: "How will I run my family. Because I was also in jail, I lost my job and there has been a lot of ostracization in the locality. I had to leave my Picnic Garden flat and move to Eliott Road. What will I do now? I am just doing some odd jobs and tuitions to keep my family afloat and you know everything has happened because of you. Please give me some money." Since then, Oluwa started giving her a few thousands every month from the drug peddling business he ran from within the prison. Meanwhile, Leeanna had befriended some of Oluwa's friends who also played football. She knew them from the parties that Oluwa had at her Picnic Garden flat before he was caught. She started sleeping with some of them, in lieu of money. Oluwa had a half-brother called Segun and Leeanna got into a relationship with him. When Oluwa got to know of this he was angry and refused to pay any more cash to Leeanna. But Leeanna kept coming every Wednesday and said sweetly: "Oh Oluwa dear, I am waiting for you to get released."

"Why I heard you have Segun now. Ask money from him."

"Who told you this lie? I just have you. Please pay my son's fees. I did not earn much this month."

Whenever anyone got ill in jail, they were taken to a doctor once in 15 days. Oluwa had gastric pain and he deliberately showed it was bad and since he knew the jailer well, he was admitted to the jail hospital. Oluwa was thus having a good time lying in bed, and having good food. Leeanna came to meet him at the hospital and Oluwa bribed the policeman who was on guard and invited Leeanna to enter his cabin. The old flame came up again and starved of sex for so many months, Oluwa literally jumped on Leeanna. Leeanna also thought this was the opportunity to please Oluwa and if she could do it, she would probably be able to extract some money from him. Thus, they made it out in that cabin.

After a few months, Leeanna's mother passed away and a bigger crisis came in. She had two elder brothers who also knew Oluwa but Leeanna did not have a good relation with them. But by then Oluwa was convinced that Leeanna was having an affair with Segun. Some of his Nigerian friends confirmed the same. So, he gave up on Leeanna and refused to pay her anymore. Leeanna too understood Oluwa would not pay her and hence decided to stop coming to the prison visits. Rather she would concentrate more on Segun and get what she needed from him.

4

Every night when Oluwa went to bed, he carried his Bible with him. Though he was a convict, he was a religious person and prayed to Lord Jesus so that his sentence is reduced. But that did not happen. He paid his lawyers too with the drug money, yet they were not of much help either. The prison became a sort of home for him. He still remembered his Nigerian wife and she had given birth to their daughter Rachel. He could not even see how she looked, there was no way that Myaka could even send him a photo. One night he was walking in the prison gardens after dinner when suddenly he saw an elderly prisoner named Narayan with a lot of cats in his cell. Oluwa got curious and went near his cell, only to be shocked. He found Narayan was having sex with a pussy cat. Deprived of sex for years, Narayan's perversion came in the form of unnatural sexual act. Oluwa felt sick seeing that and he got so angry that he pulled the man close to the door and started fisting him. Some guards came running hearing the commotion and got to know what Narayan was doing. Later counsellors were called and the jail inmates got to know that this man had tamed many cats with food and regularly had sex with them for last six years.

Then there was a gay prisoner Ahmed who would forcefully have sex with any new young prisoner who came. He would force them to have anal sex with him and also give him a blowjob. Oluwa used to laugh at his act, though Ahmed never dared to come close to this strong Nigerian. He was rather frightened of him and maintained a distance, though he preyed upon the weaker inmates. Oluwa realised there were many mini stories within the jail, no one could even imagine what crimes went on within the prison walls. Rather the guards were also paid and they behaved as if they knew nothing, just because the nexus helped in running the drug racket that fetched good money.

Meanwhile, Myaka was running her family back in Nigeria with the money that Oluwa sent and also from the grocery shop. She only knew that Oluwa was imprisoned, other family members were kept in the dark. Years went by. Patrick gave him a good lawyer and at last Oluwa's sentence was a bit reduced. He served for around 9 years and was finally released. But his release order spoke of deportation and the minute he got released, he was put on a plane back to Nigeria. He would never be allowed again to come to India. The jail life also ruined his football career, his garment business. Yet he landed in Nigeria and his wife was waiting for him.

Chapter 11

Secrets That Burn

1

As Niyaz hears the whole story, she could not believe her ears. She could not even imagine that she had not just met and fell for a criminal like Oluwa, but had an intimate physical relation with him and trusted him like anything. She was so shocked that no reaction came from her. Rather Niyaz stood up from her chair and told the coffee shop waiter to give the bill. She made the payment and left saying: "I will talk to you later."

She did not even look back or wait to see Oluwa's reaction. Niyaz was in such a shell-shocked state, that she could not go back to work. She had to think the whole thing over, alone, in q quiet place. The best place would be her house. By now the children would have returned as it was almost dusk. Yet she could say she has a bad headache and lock her bedroom and start thinking. So, she headed back home. The home that gave her a blissful sense of security, the sense of belonging to a family who had not betrayed her. She needed to take refuge there, the very home that she had left literally to be with Oluwa most afternoons at his flat enjoying wild sex. How could she do this? A wave of guilt engulfed her.

Once she reached home, she just enquired from her maid if the children had their evening snacks after returning from school. The maid replied: "Yes, I made them some *patisapta* and they enjoyed it a lot. They will have some bhuna gosht khichdi for dinner. They are now sleeping in their rooms. When the tutor comes, I will call them."

Niyaz heaved a sigh of relief. "Thank God the children are asleep, I shall have time to myself," she told herself. She took a glass of water and informed her maid that she had a bad headache and would rest now. She even added: "Do not call me even if the children wake up. I shall come out myself when I am awake. I shall now take a medicine and sleep."

As soon as she entered her sanctuary, the room that she loved and decorated herself after Naim moved into this house, Niyaz broke down. She opened all her clothes one by one and entered her bathroom to have a shower. As if the water would wipe away all her dirt and grime that had been mounting since she met Oluwa. The love and bliss that she enjoyed broke down like a pack of cards today after she got to know the real Oluwa. Why was she feeling so dirty and lost today? How could she indulge in an intimate relationship with a dirty criminal like Oluwa? Yet, a part of her was constantly asking: "Is Oluwa really a criminal?"

2

Oluwa had played with her mind and brains for sure. He had also convinced her over and over that he was not the evil man she was thinking he was. While relating his tale at the coffee shop, he had constantly repeated: "Believe me Niyaz, I have been framed. Framed by people from my country, I have no clue what was happening and why. I did not know all those false credit cards and machines were kept in a pocket in my cupboard. Leeanna knew it as it was her flat. I was just living there like a visitor as I did not have any other place to stay. I am sure she became a state witness so that she would be released scot-free and I would be put behind the bars."

Niyaz was highly sceptical. She no more could believe one word of Oluwa. She asked him: "What would Leeanna get out of that? Even if I consider she is the criminal, then why would she abandon you? You could have framed her as well. Are the police fools? Why didn't you tell them about Leeanna and your friends who you refer now to the police during interrogation. How come you are saying this now to me?"

Oluwa again pleaded: "No Niyaaz she is in hand and glove with some of my countrymen who ran the racket and also visited our apartment in Picnic Garden. I had no clue they were together hatching such a plan. I was made the victim of a bigger conspiracy."

Despite all such pleadings, Niyaaz did not believe. How could she? Her whole world with Oluwa came crumbling down. This man had deceived her, had played with her trust. Under the shower, Niyaz was crying profusely, tears of hurt and loss constantly streaming down her face. She was blaming herself. Why did I get into this relationship? Why did I betray Naim. I have committed such a sin! Here is a man who had so many relationships and a man who needed more than one woman at a time. All his life he had a constant wife, yet he kept having flings and slept around with so many women and an educated woman like me fell into his trap? How come I abandoned my own family, Naim and the kids and trusted such a promiscuous man? Will Allah ever forgive my sins?

As the cool water flowed down her bosom, Niyaz was reminded of Oluwa's touch on her naked skin. Instead of feeling aroused, Niyaz kept slapping herself to drive away even the sense of that touch. She was literally cursing herself:

"What a fool I had been! Allah, forgive me, please, please."

3

After almost half an hour, the pouring water cooled her nerves, she wore a towel over her damp body and gradually came out of the bathroom. As she was about to wear her housecoat, her phone buzzed. It was Oluwa calling. She took the call against her heart's wishes.

Oluwa sounded quite normal: "What's wrong baby? You did not reply to my messages, you are not calling?"

Niyaz angrily said: "How could you ever do such a crime and deceive me. Still, you expect me to keep in touch with you?"

"Believe me baby, I am touching my Bible and vouching that I did not do anything. I have many enemies, who wanted my career on the football fields to be doomed and then they did not even want my garments business to flourish. They connived with Leeanna to push me out of business and ruin my career. I am innocent, trust me. Please give me one more chance so that I can prove before you that I am innocent. I wish to build a family with you. Do not leave me, I am a genuine man. I love you, My Lady."

"Excuse me, family? Did you say you want to start a family with me? Are you insane?"

"Yes, I want to marry you. Leave your husband. I will stay with you and protect you."

"Really? How audacious. You don't even have any income."

"There is no hard and fast rule that a man is always a provider. I want to again start my business. You give me some capital, I promise I shall use it to do good business and earn a livelihood to return your capital and also to support you in future."

Then Oluwa went on to describe that he will set up the business in Bangladesh and stay with her. He will not return to his own country but send money for the upkeep of his children. He kept saying he will not leave her again. Niyaz was curious to know what he wanted.

And that's when his real wish was revealed. He said: "Give me 10 lakhs and I will start a uber car business at my hometown and a garment business here in Dhaka and look after you. Promise I shall never desert you. You will never again find a trustworthy man like me."

Niyaz shot back. "I have already given a lot of money to you, including your airfare to your country, airfare of so many of your business trips. I never asked you or check on you. I just trusted you blindly. Why should I pay again? How can you ask for more? Your lifestyle, your attire that you have today are mostly my gifts. I had given you gold jewellery also, including the gold chain with Jesus Christ cross on it. And you are again wanting cash?"

Niyaz at the bottom of her heart suspected for the first time that Oluwa was nothing but an extortion kingpin. Still a part of her heart was not ready to accept the truth that Oluwa was outright exploiting her. Was Niyaz so gullible? She wondered and even laughed at herself. And now she finally realised that this man was using her. Niyaz decided to take a rein on her emotions and draw a line.

She said: "Ok Oluwa I am in the middle of work. I will talk to you later. I also have a family to take care of, specially my children. I am also close to my in-laws and husband and as you know I have a big business that I single handedly run and take care of 500 workers working under me. So, they too are my responsibilities. Give me some time to get back to you. I can't promise to pay you outright."

Saying so, Niyaz disconnected the call. Now she decided to do some ground work secretly to know Oluwa's actual background and if whatever he told him about his Kolkata episode was true or not. Niyaz had some friends in Kolkata. She would need to tap them. She also decided to talk to Oluwa's brother who in the beginning had warned her about this Kolkata episode. By now Niyaz had got the name of the lawyer who had fought Oluwa's case in Kolkata and she decided to contact him too in order to get to the bottom of the whole story.

She started the investigations herself, she had completely lost trust as Oluwa was asking for money constantly. All of Oluwa's problems had now come upon her. Niyaz had actually gone to Oluwa for solace, for friendship, a shoulder to fall back on. She had no other intention. She just met Oluwa to fill in her void that was left by Naim's long absence from her life. Oluwa had entered that void and understood Niyaz was not satisfied with her husband. He used her thus giving her immense physical pleasure that she never had from her husband and in repayment he kept on using her and extorting money from her regularly. As the truth dawned on her, Niyaz felt completely devastated. A man who was a compulsive liar, who confused her, well that was Oluwa. And she will surely dig in further to get to the bottom and bring out the truth. Only then will her nerves rest.

Chapter 12

The Darker Past

1

From her sources in Kolkata, Niyaz learnt that there were several cases lodged against Oluwa, not just one for the Cash Skimming clause which he had shared with Niyaz. There were many other cases too, like cases of drug peddling and running a women trafficking racket. These were details that Oluwa did never tell Niyaz and had so long tried to prove his innocence for the credit card fraud case. What about drug handling? Women trafficking? They were equally grave offences. Niyaz's cousin sister Parveen who lived in Kolkata had met Oluwa's lawyer to get the details. Parveen had asked Niyaz: "Who is this man? How did you know him and why are you digging details on him?"

"Oh, Parveen it's a hospital case. Not a personal one. He came to be treated here and was not paying up, so my legal department were trying to hunt his previous history. Since I got to know he might have had some criminal activity that he did in Kolkata, so thought of digging further."

"Ok, but Niyaz keep away from such miscreants and ask your team never to entertain such patients."

"Yes, I will do that. Don't worry."

The lawyer gave Parveen a copy of the chargesheet and she took a photo of the same and sent it to Niyaz in case that helped in her hospital case like she had said.

2

After seeing the multiple sections under which Oluwa was booked and sent to prison, Niyaz was completely bewildered and she was trembling in fear and disgust. As she was in total shock, and just slumped on her bed, her phone rang. It was from an unknown number. May be someone from the hospital was calling. These days she hardly stayed in the hospital for long hours and even on days she did not visit her hospital. Instead, she told her secretary to take calls and only call her if it was anything urgent.

Niyaz took the call, she heard the voice of Obike on the other side. "Maam, I need to meet you. Can you give me some time?"

"Come to my hospital chamber. I shall meet you there." Niyaz had no clue what Obike wished to tell her and hence she did not wish to entertain him anywhere else. Not just that she had a faint apprehension that Oluwa had sent Obike to talk her out. So, she decided the hospital would be a neutral and safe place to meet.

Next day Obike came to her office and she offered him coffee. Niyaz was a very decent woman and she would not allow her anger or sorrow to be expressed. Yet she was looking so stressed and down for last few days that it did not miss Obike's watch and he asked: "Is everything OK with you? I find Oluwa also very restless these days. Have you both had a fight?"

Niyaz at first did not reply. Rather she asked him to have his coffee. Then slowly she opened up: "Obike, I need to ask you something. But before that you have to promise me that you will tell me the truth."

"Yes, I shall tell you the truth for sure."

"Tell me things about Oluwa that you know. I want his details."

"You better then ma'am, tell me whatever you know and then I shall tell you what more I know."

Niyaz was irritated at Obike's audacity and said: "Listen Obike, we are not playing word games here. I have real concern to know about Oluwa and I think I have every right to know. You being his cousin, am sure you know him better than I do. And tell me the truth and whatever I need to know or not need to know, tell me everything about Oluwa's past."

3

Obike now took a backseat and turned serious. "I respect you ma'am but what much will I talk about Oluwa. I am sure by now you know about his criminal past. Yes, definitely he was in prison and for many years he was confined for money laundering and fraud charges. Quite naturally he is a changed man now because if any man stays in prison for almost a decade, then his attitude changes. He can no more be the same man. Oluwa was not like this before, believe me ma'am. He is now more like an animal. His nature has completely changed. He is no more the man I knew long back. He has changed with time, from the stress and anxiety he had while in prison. He is now more inhuman."

"What about his relationships with women?" Niyaz enquired.

"He had many women in his life but he never deserted his wife. This much I know."

"But Obike, your brother is now proposing to marry me and wants to stay with me and start a family. Also, I have given him huge sums of money as help. What exactly he wants from me? Money, sex or family?"

"I would say if you are with Oluwa, just enjoy him. Do not get mentally involved with him. Else you will break down one day. You are a matured woman ma'am and I know he will never leave his wife. He has never done that even when he had relations with other women. They were like his side kicks, but his wife is his children's mother, he will never leave her come what may. In Nigeria they have their own family and house. And maam, you also have a business to run, kids and a husband. Why will you leave them to be with Oluwa! I am really surprised that Oluwa has told you such things. But I shall advise you to take the decision very wisely."

Niyaz nodded her head. She was in deep thought and Obike asked for leave as he had to go to work. As he was leaving, Niyaz called back: "Please keep today's discussion to yourself. I hope I can trust you."

"Yes maam, I will. I respect you and you have every right to decide on your life." Saying that Obike left the room.

4

Niyaz was now alone and started reflecting on her life. Many queries crisscrossed her mind. 'Was I in a spell?' Obike had told her that Oluwa and his wife, both practiced voodoo or black magic and have been partners for years. Even when he was in prison, Leeanna left him, but his wife was with him and even encouraged him to run a drug business from within the prison so that he could send money home. Oluwa loved Leeanna and his son too, but somehow, she understood on time that she was being exploited and quietly moved away when he was sent to prison and when she realised this man would be of no use to her as well.

For Niyaz it was the other way round. She was the giver, constantly giving to Oluwa, expecting nothing in return. Now she questioned herself, what was my role then in Oluwa's life? Well, I need to sit back and get away too. Meanwhile, Oluwa kept messaging and calling her. She started avoiding him. One day while in her chamber, she called Naim in England and spoke for a long time. Naim was surprised.

He asked: "What a surprise! I thought you are busy."

Niyaz brushed aside the sarcasm in his tone and instead said: "The children's vacation will start in a few months' time. I am planning to take them to England with me and we as a family can stay there for a month or so. What do you say?"

It was news to Naim. Despite asking Niyaz to come and settle in UK since long or even come and visit, she had always avoided giving the hospital duties as an excuse. And now she was wanting on her own to come down. Naim was a bit happy at this and immediately declared: "Wow, that would be great. I shall plan in advance where all we can take the kids for a visit in UK. They will have a blast. It is also Christmas time and England looks beautiful. They can have a great time shopping Santa and Christmas trees.

"Ok Naim I will tell the kids of this plan tonight. Am sure they will feel excited and you can book our air tickets now so that you will get some discount."

Naim agreed and felt happy. Niyaz kept the phone down and again started wondering about Oluwa. Somehow, she could not drive him from her head. She laid down on the couch in her chamber and looked up at the ceiling. Unknowingly, uncontrolled tears rolled down. She could not stop crying despite knowing this was her official space and her secretary could enter any minute. This man had used her so badly. Yet, she had a sense of love still lingering for him. Why? She was herself confused at her own feelings. She still looked for his messages, the curiosity to look him up on social media posts still lingered, some sort of eagerness that kept nudging her. Was it love? Was it sex? Or companionship? Or was it friendship? Niyaz had no answer to her thoughts.

Chapter 13

Love or Illusion?

1

It was a Monday morning at the hospital and Niyaz was neck deep in work with her Accounts team. Md Hafiz who was her Chartered Accountant heading the hospital finance team had booked slots over the week to sit with Niyaz and the mountain load of accounts. The hospital was new and hence in the first few years every financial transaction had to be looked into many times so that the books were up to date and the auditors found no faults. Niyaz had worked hard to bring the hospital to this height and one wrong step could jeopardise all her expansion plans.

Over the past few weeks Niyaz had pushed Oluwa out of her head, so as to concentrate on this work and had deliberately asked Hafiz Sir and his team to meet her multiple times. Like a bruised woman, a woman whose love was lost or killed in war, Niyaz was literally trying to put a balm to her wounds. She was an emotional woman and had deeply fallen in love with Oluwa. But the way his past revealed, Niyaz was shattered and could not forgive herself for trusting a wrong man. Yet a part of her yearned for his touch, and refused to believe that the man who once upon a time showed her so much love and respect was actually a hardened criminal? Or was he not? The tug of war that Niyaz was thrown into, a war where she was the lone warrior and could not share the real story with any other soul under the sun made Niyaz vulnerable. Yet she stood her ground and like always decided to drown herself in loads of work that would help her to forget the betrayal to some extent. She would now spend more time with the hospital staff, with her children, and even visited her mother-in-law who was surprised to know that she would soon be joining Naim in London on a vacation with the kids.

She had blessed Niyaz over and over saying: "Thank God, you have at last realised you need to be with your husband."

"I am only going for a vacation. And will definitely enjoy."

"You better think of going permanently. Naim is having a lot of trouble cooking all by himself."

"Well, Naim never told me that."

"He will never tell you, you are the learned and more prosperous wife, not a mere housewife like us and hence Naim keeps you on a high pedestal always. But that does not mean you will take advantage of his goodness."

While returning to the hospital from her in-laws' house, one word kept swirling in her mind. Did she really take advantage of Naim's goodness and cheated her husband to be with Oluwa? A wave of remorse hit her and she burnt from within, flames that would not be doused soon, she knew, at least it could be pushed under a carpet. And that's what she would be doing, getting into the hospital matter first hand, something that she ignored off late while she was giving time to Oluwa. She would change. She kept telling herself: "I must come out of this. I must." The lines of struggle shone on her face.

2

Meanwhile Oluwa could not contact Niyaz at all. She had not taken his calls for weeks and not even replied to his constant messages. He could understand she had seen and read the messaged on whatsapp as the blue ticks appeared, but she never replied. So, on Monday, the very day Niyaz sat with her accounts team, Oluwa decided to meet her at the hospital. When he reached, Niyaz's secretary who already knew Oluwa well said: "Maam is very busy, the audit of our hospital is on and she is with the accounts team, I do not think she has time to meet any guests today." That was a standard dialogue she gave to most guests, though Oluwa so long had been a special guest and was always given a royal welcome by her madam. At least the secretary had observed that but her maam had categorically told her not to allow Oluwa at all.

Yet Oluwa was not to be deterred. He said: "Ok I am waiting, let your maam finish the audit, I shall meet her after that." Saying so, Oluwa sat on the big sofa at the reception area. The secretary had no other alternative, but to call her madam. "Maam sorry to disturb you, but Mr Oluwa is here and is refusing to leave without meeting you."

Niyaz was so engrossed with the ledgers and the team that at first nothing registered her. She asked: "Who has come?"

"Mr Oluwa madam, that big African guy."

The words suddenly hit Niyaz like the gust of wind and she sat up straight. Concealing the sudden rush of emotional distress and the colour rising in her cheeks, Niyaz said: "I have no time, ask him to wait if he wants to and tell him I have no clue how long he has to wait, it can be 1-2 hours also. I shall not meet anyone till I finish my job."

"OK maam, conveying your message to him." As the secretary put down the phone, Niyaz heaved a sigh. Was it of a relief that she could ward off the man for some hours or was it a sigh of hidden grief? Md Hafiz who was a fatherly man looked up and asked staring at Niyaz's sudden pale face: "Anything wrong?"

Niyaz immediately controlled herself and said: "No Hafiz chacha, it is a patient issue and he has come to meet me. I asked the man to wait."

While working, Niyaz had lost the track of time. Suddenly, Oluwa barged in, peeping through the door, by pushing the same. "Hello Maam."

Niyaz was visibly irritated, seeing him in the middle of an official meeting with senior officials. She looked up and said with a lot of effort: "Please wait outside. Who allowed you to come in?" The rest of the team also stared at the tall Afro man, little understanding what was going on. Oluwa realised he needed to step back. So, he nodded and closed the door.

Md Hafiz spoke up: "Beti who is this man? He looks so menacing."

"Hafiz chacha this is the patient I spoke of." Saying so, she called up her secretary and the phone kept ringing. She looked angry. "No clue why these people leave their desk and allow visitors to just barge in!"

Within five minutes, the secretary called back: "Yes maam, you called?"

"How come this man Mr Oluwa walked into my room unannounced. Where were you?" Niyaz sounded a bit rude, a big deviation from her ways.

"Maam I was in the washroom and may be during that time he went in taking advantage of my absence," the secretary sounded alarmed.

"Then ask him to leave or he has to wait for few more hours. If he chooses to wait, give him a cup of coffee."

But Oluwa refused to leave. He would meet Niyaz today at any cost. The meeting continued for hours and though

Oluwa had always been impatient and always considered himself as a boss man, he diligently kept waiting. Was it out of love? Or was it because of a need, the need for money? Would he again try to exploit her?

3

Finally, the meeting was over and Hafiz and his team left. Niyaz composed herself, went to the washroom, put on some make up and called up her secretary.

"Is Mr Oluwa still waiting?" A part of her, infact wished he did wait.

"Yes maam, he is still here. Should I send him in?"

"Yes, please do so."

She sat back in her chair more officially as Oluwa entered with a dazzling smile just like old times. "Hi beautiful. So, these days you have forgotten me?"

Niyaz was amazed at the cheek of the man. He was behaving as if nothing happened. She said in a serious tone: "Sit." And then she went on to say: "Tell me why you wanted to meet?"

In a very emotive tone, as if heartbroken beyond words, Oluwa asked, bending over to her: "Is everything over between you and me? Just because I have a bitter past, so you are rejecting me My Lady?"

There was so much yearning in that voice that Niyaz stifled. For a minute she did not know how to react. A part of her felt like forgetting everything and embracing him like before. A fire rose in her groins, every episode of their sexual encounters, that Niyaz had taken with dollops of love, played before her eyes. But she had to stop. She had to draw a final line.

In a matter-of-fact way, she replied: "I don't know if there was anything between us or if now, we have anything between us but between your black and white questions there are many grey lines and I want to know those grey lines. I have many unanswered questions Oluwa and until I am sure of their answers, I cannot go back to the form as if nothing went wrong."

Now Oluwa shouted, something he hardly ever did. "What more do you want to know? Didn't I tell you enough?" He was visibly dejected at Niyaz's refusal to go back to their previous relationship.

But this anger did not impact Niyaz, unlike the time when she was slapped by Oluwa. Over past few weeks, she had done a lot of introspection and the part of her that got carried away with Oluwa, finally found peace. Calmly Niyaz answered: "So you have only one criminal offence against you? That is money laundering or credit card fraud? Don't you have any other offence? Like drug peddling? Women racketing?"

"No nothing happened, someone is misleading you about the charges against me," Oluwa lied through his teeth. Niyaz took out some papers from the drawer on her desk that her sister had sent from Kolkata. She threw the stack on the desk and asked: "So all these are lies? So many chargesheets against you?"

Oluwa hadn't expected he would be confronted with proof and hence was a bit unnerved at first. But quickly he took charge and banged his fist on the papers on the table and said: "Yes, they are all false. These are false papers and charges. There is a conspiracy against me and hence all these false cases were filed against me. There were a bunch of people working against me and they were unable to frame me in any of the cases whose paper you are showing now.

Finally, they could charge me in the credit card fraud case, that too I was not involved in and put me to prison."

4

Niyaz obviously did not believe this story and said: "Listen Oluwa, you are wanting money from me again. But I have taken a decision. Henceforth there will be no money transaction between you and me. I have done enough for you and asking nothing in return. I have a limit to which I can help you financially and I do not owe you anything that I need to keep giving you money. I am answerable to few people in my life too. So, from now on there will be no money exchange between us. If you need food or clothes etc, I will buy and give you. But money should not come between us and we can be friends beyond that. Consider if you like my proposal, then we can keep in touch, else not."
Oluwa sat back with a lot of sorrow in his eyes and stared at Niyaz for a few minutes --- the lapse of time that sent a multitude of feelings through Niyaz. Did she do this right? Is she being too harsh? What if he was telling the truth? What if he was really framed by his friends? What if he really loved her, and would fill the void she had with Naim?

She was jolted from her thoughts, as Oluwa replied: "Ok if money is creating a problem, fair enough, I will not ask for any financial help from you." He spoke in such an authoritarian manner, as if he was doing a great favour to Niyaz by not asking for money.

"By the way, I also need some space. Please do not flood my inbox with hundreds of messages or keep calling me. If I am not answering, it means I am busy. Hope you will respect that. I shall require some time to gulp in the revelations about you that has happened over past one month."

Oluwa now became defensive. "What is there to gulp in Maam? What will I gain telling lies to you? I am repeatedly telling you that I was framed. I am not the criminal that you think I am. Why are you not trusting me?"

"This is not a question of gain or loss. It's about love and emotions. But you will not understand as you are like a stone after so many years of imprisonment." These were the exact words of Obike. Niyaz repeated those words, he had informed her how being in the prison with bad people for years had changed Oluwa. How his habits turned rotten, how he had become more violent and emotionless and a different man. "And by the way you had hit me, have you forgotten that Oluwa? It is unpardonable. In our country men do not beat their wives or any other woman."

"Well, I said sorry for that."

"Sorry doesn't mend everything. As I said before there are several grey areas in our relationship and I need to address them. We can start afresh like friends. You cannot leave your wife and I also cannot leave my husband and children. So, we can be friends, provided I feel you are trustworthy."

Oluwa nodded, like a defeated player on a football field who lost a game after the final whistle. He added now in an official tone: "Today I had come to discuss with you about a new business I am launching with a friend from India, Manish More. I did not come for money or sex. I came to discuss that business venture with you. Your family owns a shopping mart. Can you keep some of our goods in your mart?"

The question hung in the air, as Niyaz's secretary walked in to inform: "Maam your team is waiting for you at the lunch table. Will you be late."

Niyaz got up. "No, I am coming with you." Then turning to Oluwa she said: "Ok bye Mr Oluwa. We shall connect over your business proposal about Paisa Bazar later this week. You can make an appointment with my secretary in advance." Saying so, she walked out of her chamber and did not even look back for once.

Chapter 14

The Fraudulent Dream

1

Manish More lived in Mumbai and with him Oluwa decided to start a mobile phone business. They would buy the machines from China and sell it to the cheaper markets. Accordingly, Oluwa got busy doing the market survey in different parts of Bangladesh. The semi-rural areas of Bangladesh could be a good place to sell these Chinese phones. Oluwa instantly understood the pulse of the market. Meanwhile, Manish and his other partner Yogesh went to China and signed an agreement with a Chinese company who would send their products to Oluwa in Bangladesh and from there the phones would be shipped to other countries like Myanmar, Taiwan and Nigeria, where there was a big emerging market for such phones. From China, Manish and Yogesh came to Dhaka to meet Oluwa. They were staying in a 5-star hotel near the city centre, quite close to Niyaz's hospital.

One day Oluwa called Niyaz on her hospital number, fearing that she would not take his mobile call. She said: "Two of my friends cum business partners have come from India. They would love to meet you. Can we meet at some hotel for lunch or dinner or even at a coffee shop as per your convenience?" Oluwa sounded sugary sweet, unlike their last meeting.

But Niyaz had become stricter, though her soft corner for this man with whom she shared many moments still remained. She said: "No you can come to my office. We can discuss whatever your business partners wish to tell me." Oluwa did not argue further. He was really keen that Manisha and Yogesh meet Niyaz so as to convince her to help them market the product in Bangladesh. Oluwa had realised by then that his own words were no more effective enough to convince Niyaz. Hence, he was keen to take his partners for the meeting.

2

As Manish lived in Kolkata for many years, he could speak in Begali quite a bit as well as in English. While talking, Niyaz was reminded of the names on the chargesheets that her sister had sent. Didn't she see Manish's name too? Though the charge against him was not too dire and he was released on bail soon. Yet he was himself a crime suspect in Oluwa's racket that he ran in India and particularly in West Bengal. So Niyaz got a bit more guarded in her conversation with Oluwa's partners.

"Who all do you have in your family?" she asked Manish.

"My wife and kids."

Before he could finish or go on to describe further, Oluwa added: "I know his wife since long. When Manish lived in Mumbai, I visited a couple of times. I used to stay in his Mumbai flat. They are one big happy family."

Niyaz silently listened to everything. She was trying to add up the missing links and was in constant search of the truth that she had wanted to know about Oluwa from day 1. Her thoughts were broken when Manish said: "I have heard a lot from Oluwa about you and he always praises you. So, what are your plans? You and Oluwa?"

Niyaz was surprised. She shot back: "What plans? We are just good friends. What plans can we have?" In the bottom of her heart, Niyaz prayed that Oluwa had not gone around telling his so-called friends and partners that she slept with him. Or did he? How far had Oluwa revealed about their relationship? Niyaz wondered. Else how could Manish be so audacious to ask about their life together, as if she was about to marry Oluwa!

Oluwa realised Niyaz was uneasy. He butted in: "Oh come on Manish, we shall plan once our business takes off." Niya felt Oluwa must have given Manish some false background about their relation. Manish invited Niyaz courteously to the 5-star hotel where he was staying, over lunch someday. Niyaz took leave and decided not to indulge these men further and waste her time in their company.

3

The phones finally arrived from China and they named it Skywalk. Skywalk was launched in a very big way in one of the biggest shopping plazas of Dhaka. In every newspaper of Bangladesh, both English and vernacular as well as on TV channels, they gave ads about this great yet cheap mobile phone. Manish's target was to get into the semi-urban and rural markets of Bangladesh, where population was high, yet they would wish to use cheaper phones.

Oluwa kept pestering Niyaz to buy phones and keep them on display at their Supermarket. The Supermarket was owned by Niyaz's in-laws and though she was in the board of directors, she did not wish to take undue advantage and told Oluwa: "I have to ask other board members and our sales team. I just cannot do a favour to you just because you are asking for it. Only if everyone agrees to keep the phone, we can try to display some phones."

To convince her further, Oluwa sent Yogesh one afternoon to her hospital to give a detailed presentation about their phone and how user friendly it was. Yogesh tried to sell the products to Niyaz and he was so convincing that Niyaz finally called the tech team to assess if they were worth keeping. Oluwa went a step further. He requested: "Niyaz for old time's sake, why don't you buy some phones, say just 5 of them and keep them? I am sure they will sell like hot cakes and once they do, you can order for more. Just 5. Can't you do this little for us?"

The phones were quite costly, infact their price was at par with many international branded phones. "I cannot decide alone, we have to look into the budget." Niyaz was at a loss as to how to avoid them. But she knew it would be difficult, they wanted a presence at their shopping mart which was centrally located and was quite popular.

To influence her further, Manish even gifted her a phone and said: "As a gift I am giving this to you. Just use it and find out for yourself how good they are!"

Niyaz was impressed by Manish's gesture, though she was sceptical whether to accept the gift or not. Finally, she did, though Niyaz already used a high-end international model that Naim had gifted her last summer. The sales were going well and Niyaz's tech team gave a go ahead to the phone. Accordingly, the sales team paid fifty thousand and kept a few phones at their display counter. Skywalk was doing well, they were selling everywhere and the trio were making quick profits. Manish, Yogesh and Oluwa were dividing the money amongst themselves.

4

One day Oluwa said: "Let us party tonight and celebrate this launch at my place."

Niyaz however again drew a line and refused to visit his apartment. Wasn't it the same place from where she had stormed out one day. She didn't wish to go back there again. It is said that memories can play a dirty game and hence Niyaz thought it would be best to meet elsewhere. She said: "No, not today. Manish has already invited me over lunch at his hotel, I shall try and make it one day. His hotel and my hospital are close by." Niyaz somehow liked the soft-spoken Manish. He was a family man and very courteous in his ways, unlike the rough and tough Oluwa. Oluwa's machoism no more appealed to a broken heart.

Days and weeks passed in a busy humdrum. Both Niyaz and Oluwa were working in their own spheres. His messages were lesser now. Niyaz still expected messages from him, but why? Why did she still have expectations? Was her love for him still alive? She diverted her mind and did not bother much. She realised there was no end to this, feelings tumbled out on their own, she had to control. She tried to move out of Oluwa's charm gradually, but her mental attachment was so high that it was difficult for her to move out fast. She still impatiently waited for him at times, specially on sleepless nights when she remained awake alone, thinking of her times with Oluwa.

The phones that Oluwa sent to Nigeria, his wife and brother kept some in their store. Niyaz at times wondered from where Oluwa and the others got license for cross continent business. She wondered did they again commit some fraud? For such ventures a lot of legal papers were needed. They took an office in Basundhara of Dhaka and

Oluwa even got a car and promoted the product by travelling in it far and wide. Niyaz gave him some references also and they were giving a lot of offers and opened many small outlets all across Bangladesh specially targeting the Tier 2 cities. People started buying the products and even the ones kept at Niyas's supermarket were sold out. Though the supermarket usually kept branded products and did not keep Chinese made products, but thanks to the supermarket, Skywalk found place alongside well-known brands.

Money was trickling in and the partners were earning well. Oluwa kept sending back all his earnings home. He did not even bother to buy anything at all for Niyaz or give back some of the money that she had given him earlier.

One day after a lot of persuasion, Niyaz finally met Manish at his hotel. Oluwa was also around and talking to Yogesh, standing at the gate, while Niyaz and Manish were at the bar, enjoying some beverages. Manish was drinking and Niyaz could not hold her curiosity any longer. She asked him:

"How do you know Oluwa?"

Manish said: "Oh! Oluwa, he is a colourful man. You must be knowing too. What a big fraud he is! I was also charge sheeted in a fraud case due to him." He was drinking and so he was in a half stupor.

"I heard he was betrayed?" Niyaz asked innocently. Did she then still believe in Oluwa's story?

Manish laughed. "Come on Niyaz, you are so naïve. No one has the guts to betray Oluwa. He will kill them. He is like an animal."

Niyaz was tempted further to ask: "Do you know his wife and family?"

"Oh yes, I have been to his house in Nigeria, we had a garment business together. His wife is a typical rural woman and they have a wonderful relationship."

"Is she a prophetess?"

"What' that? No clue. But she treated us well, fed us their traditional food. They have their own house, quite a big one."

"Rest of the family?"

By then Manish was almost wasted. "I do not know Niyaz and I have no wish to know. I just know he gets a steady supply of money from somewhere always, he was into a number of fraud rackets and unfortunately, I got embroiled in one and have a case hanging against me still in India! What about you? Are you his partner?"

Niyaz could not tolerate the conversation any longer. She left in a huff bidding good night to Manish. She took the other door to the exit, so that she wouldn't have to meet Oluwa or Yogesh.

Chapter 15

The Final Goodbye

1

The date to travel to London neared and Niyaz was busy packing. Her children's vacations would soon kick off and she had to give all instructions to her hospital staff too, so that in her month-long absence the hospital ran smoothly. Her medical super Dr Kabir Huda had multiple meetings with her and so did her secretary who would be in constant touch with her in case anything urgent needed to be addressed.

Meanwhile, her mother-in-law had packed some food items that were Naim's favourite and she was overjoyed that the kids would soon meet their father.

"Oh! Niyaz I am so happy. Please see to it that over this month you stay there, you cook payesh and firni. They are my son's favourite. I am sure he doesn't get to eat all this."

"There are several Bangladeshi food outlets in the area Naim stays. It is near the Scotland borders. Do not worry. Am sure he gets warm meals that reminds him of his home."

Still her mother-in-law was not impressed. "How can you say that Niyaz. He stays thousands of miles away from us and he deserves a good home cooked meal daily. Just because you refused to leave your hospital, he is staying alone in a foreign land. Do you know how worried I am? It's all your fault."

By now Niyaz was used to such allegations by her mother-in-law. She had never found anything worthy in her. On the contrary she was very cozy to her elder son's wife who was a perfect home maker and always tried to please her. Her younger son Naim had got an educated woman as wife, and that's where all problem started. That's how Niyaz's mother-in-law had taken a dislike to her from the beginning.

Meanwhile, Naim had already sent the tickets and visas were done. Niyaz's travel agent was very efficient and he had been with them since her father's time. Hafizul chacha was also happy that she was going to her husband. He came to handover the visa and passports stamped and blessed her saying: "Beti I am so happy you are going to your husband after so many months. Enjoy your trip."

Niyaz somehow had a feeling that this world would accept her only when she was in her husband's arms. The pretty little perfect family picture --- that's what the world always wished to see. Niyaz also feels excited to some extent as she realised a change of place would definitely help her get over the trauma that she felt within due to Oluwa's criminal background revelation. A part of her wished to run away and forget what all happened, while another part of her felt sorry for Oluwa. How could a man who had so much love once upon a time, be a hardened criminal? Was that possible? What a dichotomy! Yet she knew she loved the man and her subconscious always yearned for his touch. So long she hadn't informed Oluwa of her London trip and that she had planned a month back. She would eventually tell him, that was her plan.

2

On Monday morning Naim's elder brother Waqar came with all food packets that his mother had planned to send to London. While having a cup of tea at Niyaz's house, he suddenly said: "Niyaz I forgot to tell you something. The other day, a customer who had bought the Skywalk phone which you had asked me to keep on display asked about the service centre. Please ask your vendor to send me the address."

"Oh! OK. Will ask. I had not thought of this before, the marketing team should have asked."

"Yes, I asked your marketing team. They also have no clue. They said since you said it is your friend who is doing the business, they didn't bother much to ask. Even if international products are sold, they too have service centres here. Else how will buyers get after sales service. Also ask him about the license papers. We need to ensure they are not counterfeit or duplicate products. As you know our supermarket has a reputation for keeping the best brands." Niyaz nodded, a deep thoughtful expression in her eyes. "I will get back to you, and thanks Waqar Bhai for all the gifts you sent for the kids last month. They really loved them." As soon as Waqar left, Niyaz immediately called Oluwa. He didn't take the call.

She left a message: "Call back, its urgent."

Oluwa called after an hour and in a sugary sweet voice said: "Oh I am so lucky my lady. After months you have finally called me. It must be my lucky day."

Without giving attention to whatever Oluwa was saying, Niyaz continued: "The product you are selling, where is the license and what is the after sales service you are offering."

Suddenly there was a silence on the other end. And then Manish's voice came in. Oluwa had transferred the phone conveniently to Manish. "Hi maam it is a Chinese product and as of now there are no sales office in Bangladesh but they would soon open sales offices and service centres here. Do not worry. If any of your customers ask such questions send them to our Basundhara office. I will explain. And maam would you like to buy a few more sets?"

Niyaz knew she did not get the answer to the question she asked. She said: "Not now, will let you know if we have any query."

Niyaz then dialled Waqar's number and told him what Manish related. Waqar being a businessman since many years and looking after multiple ventures set by his father, realised there was something amiss in the whole transaction. He was somehow not convinced by Manish's words and said: "Niyaz one thing, do not buy any more phones. We shall also not showcase these products anymore. I think these are counterfeit products. We cannot jeopardise our reputation and get into any legal tangle."

"Ok bhai. I will keep that in mind." Niyaz was feeling disturbed. Did Oluwa and Manish again start a duping business? She blamed herself for falling in their trap again. It's said love has its own ways and did that very love blind an educated woman like Niyaz? She should have questioned Oluwa before buying the products.

3

As the day of her departure came closer, Niyaz called Oluwa and informed him that she would be away for a little more than a month. "I will take my kids to my husband in London. I shall be leaving early next week. Thought of informing you."

"Oh really, you did not tell me earlier. How come you are leaving without telling me, I had no clue about your plans." Oluwa sounded possessive.

"Well, you are busy with your new business. I was busy with my hospital audit. I had a plan long ago to go, Naim had been asking since months."

Oluwa said in a pleading voice: "Before you leave, please meet me one last time."

There was so much emotion in his voice that Niyaz could not say no. She said: "Come to my office then." Oluwa came the very next day. He almost was on his knees with a rose in his hand. "Will miss you so much dearest. Come back fast." Then he kissed her suddenly and then tried to caress her hands and back. Niyaz was not prepared for this outburst. Despite the warmth of love she had harboured for him in his heart, she had turned cold and said: "Please Oluwa. This is my office. Go and sit."

Oluwa looked perplexed. Niyaz and he had met in her office previously too but she never behaved thus. "Why suddenly this change?" he asked. And then finding Niyaz silent to his query, he said: "When will you be back?"
"Not sure. Will let you know. My return tickets are still not booked."

"Hope you are coming back. Or are you settling there?" Oluwa asked in a suspicious voice.

Niyaz smiled a bit and replied: "I will be back. We shall meet again."

4

Naim was waiting excitedly outside the airport for his family. The sight of his kids after so many months made him rush forward like a child. He embraced them dearly. Niyaz gave a warm smile at the sight. Naim had been a very affectionate father always and Niyaz loved that part of his. No wonder even while she was with Oluwa, her respect for

Naim and the need of keeping the family close, never left her. She knew this family was very important for her. Naim had a lovely house with a wonderful garden. He had arranged for breakfast and lunch in advance at a local Bangladeshi restaurant. The first few days he will not allow Niyaz to cook. He took care of everything. Naim too missed his family and he wanted to go out of his way to prove to Niyaz how good a husband he was and what a nice place he lived in. In case Niyaz changed her mind and relocated!

Over the past one-month Oluwa had earned a lot by selling the phone sets. But these were sets imported from China without any valid import license and they were all duplicate products which they were selling. Initially no one got a hang of it as they had advertised Skywalk so much along the length and breadth of Dhaka that consumers got attracted and bought in hordes. But once they started asking for after sales service as most of the phones were having problems, then they realised there were no service centres of Skywalk.

Many consumers thus filed cases in court or consumer's forum against Oluwa and Manish's company that were selling through distributors. By then Oluwa had also sent many handsets to Nigeria for his brother and wife to sell them. But now the sales had to stop. They tried to sell in some local shops, that was not possible as well as no one would buy such products that were costly, everyone demanded valid papers. Manish realised this would be a big problem and hence without a word he returned to India with whatever money he had earned. Meanwhile Oluwa got stranded in Dhaka as his visa got lapsed and he forgot to extend it. Renewal of visas for Africans in Bangladesh was not easy and now that the police got a wind of their counterfeit mobile phone business, with hundreds of complaints trickling down, they issued an arrest warrant against Oluwa.

Oluwa fled to Myanmar via road but there too he could not stay long. He had to return to Dhaka and the police had already launched a massive manhunt. There was no way that he could avert the police arrest. Oluwa was fined and deported to Nigeria, literally penniless. He tried to contact Niyaz as he was confident that she would help him. But once in UK, Niyaz had changed her sim to a local number. She did not try to contact Oluwa while in UK with Naim and even blocked him on her social media etc deleting all chats, so that Naim would never get to know of Oluwa. She could not jeopardise her family life for she knew Naim would divorce her if he had any suspicion of another man in her life.

A month later when Niyaz returned home, she switched back to her previous number and dialled Oluwa's number. Every time it said 'out of service.' So Niyaz called Obike. She had a hunch that Oluwa probably was deported for his fraudulent business just like he was done in India. Obike said: "Maam I cannot say everything on phone. I need to come and meet you."

The very next day he came to her office and related the whole story. "Maam, he tried to contact you several times. We could not help him too, as if the police got to know we are helping, they might have deported us too. You know how harsh Bangladeshi police is on foreigners like us. The saddest part is after returning to Nigeria, Oluwa had a massive cerebral stroke and was in bed for weeks. One side of his is paralysed."

Niyaz could not believe her ears. That huge masculine man, who had once held her in deep embrace, was confined to bed!

"Can I speak to him Obike? Please?"

"Yes maam, I am calling from my WA and connecting you."

As the line connected, Niyaz literally snatched the phone from Obike and said: "Oluwa I am so sorry to hear about your health. How are you now?"

Oluwa said in a feeble voice: "You were not there when I was in huge trouble Niyaz. You were not there. I was alone. No one was there for me. I am being given back by God for my sins."

"Don't talk like that Oluwa. Just tell me how are you now?"

"I am a pauper now."

"Try something new in Nigeria, I know you cannot come back to Bangladesh."

"What will I try Niyaz. I still have 100 pieces of those phones with me. I tried to sell them here. No one is taking, everyone asks for papers. You know it was Manish and Yogesh who went to China. I didn't, tell me Niyaz how will I know that they were buying duplicate assembled phones without papers."

"Oluwa forget about the phones. Try to increase your garment business. Gain and loss are part of life."

"I have no money left and I am now confined to bed, a burden to all. I loved you Niyaz, believe me I did. But God didn't want us to stay together. We come from different cultures and backgrounds, yet we were one, weren't we? All those moments I spent with you Niyaz, I keep thinking of them, now that I cannot do much physical work. Lying in bed, I think of you. Only you. And I am not telling a lie. You probably think I am a criminal. But my love is pure. It is for you and you only."

Niyaz almost lost her voice. She said softly: "Keep in touch Oluwa. We shall probably meet someday again. Who knows?"

She disconnected. And started sobbing, uncontrolled tears streaming down her face. She no more cared that it was her office space and that Obike was sitting right infront of her. At times it is hard to do what the world thinks right and what the society dictates. Niyaz's heart for once ruled over her head.

Acknowledgements

I am indebted to the correctional homes in India and Bangladesh for having me as a consultant, psychologist and counselling the convicts of life and long imprisonments. I thank my family, my husband, my kids and my parents and sister for supporting and motivating me to pen this real-life experiential book. I would also like to thank Saheli Mitra and her Content & Creative company Tales Talks Walks for editing and designing this book. Lastly, I am grateful to the universe and my life which has imparted me with numerous lessons and chapters and presented both setbacks and tools of improvisation. I thank God for giving me all the challenges and moments of breaking apart as they helped me to grow more mature and discover myself as a better empowered human being.